I0569755

Stripped

Book 1: Muddy Heels

By
Jayne Dixon

Wooden Stake Press
Denver, CO

What other people are saying about "Stripped":

"Well, I just read it all in one sitting because I couldn't put it down! Loving it!"

"This story is a fun romp through the world of an average girl finding her place of belonging within an average strip club, but with TONS of fun, sexiness, adventure, mystery, lust, love, and plot twists! It is wonderfully written and will keep you turning pages with excitement, then at the end, leave you breathless and ready for the sequel."

"The sexual tension is unbearable!"

"You are an amazing writer. Thank you for blessing me and giving me an escape."

"I was absorbed in this book from the moment it finished downloading onto my iPad, and I didn't put it down until I was done! The relationships are complex and intriguing; the writing strikes the perfect balance between evocative scene-setting and plot moving, and the sexy scenes are written in a way that allowed me to almost live vicariously through Ellie."

"Intense…"

Also by Jayne Dixon:

Losing You (Book 1)

Keeping You (Book 2)

Saving Me (Book 3)

Coming Soon:

Stripped
Book 2: Bloody Heels

For my amazing husband who has supported the creative process and all of my quirky writers' habits so I could see this dream come alive. And for my kids who put up with a very spacey mom during moments of inspiration!

A special thanks to my beta readers who built an insane level of excitement over this book and pushed me to finish it (you know who you are)!

CONTENTS

Stripped

Chapter 1

I clutch my leather satchel with a tension that turns my knuckles white; and I haven't even gotten to my gate yet. My anxiety is eclipsed by every well-toned, brown-haired man that enters my peripheral vision – as if I'm watching the final results of the power ball tease their way into place.

I suppose the typical airport smells of cinnamon rolls and Mexican food is delightful enough when the rum-infused breath of the drunken man next to me isn't abusing my senses. Every few minutes, he burps loudly without reservation and takes another gulp from his 'coffee' cup. It's like I'm back in college again, watching my Chemistry professor grade papers, the sweat from his rolling neck dripping across the keyboard while his stained yellow teeth made a disturbing clicking sound. If I had any choice in the matter, I wouldn't hesitate to offer this drunkard the entire bench; he could certainly use the space. But as it is, I'm stuck

1

here, my fingers sweaty and twitching while my eyes dart from person to person hoping that this ridiculous daydream I'm chasing isn't as elusive as it seems. If this man weren't so tantalizing; if he hadn't made me burn in ways I'd never experienced, I might never have stepped foot in another airport. But I'm hard pressed to come up with any reason not to do as he requests, especially when the possibilities are endlessly appealing.

I miss dancing already: the smooth movements, the adrenaline pulsating through my veins, the hot and horny clientele shouting at me over the bumping dance mix. Everywhere else in the world leaves a lot to be desired. Stressed out travelers, screaming children, and overworked fast food employees are equally boisterous, but there is certainly no pleasure to be had within a mile of where I sit.

For what God-awful reason am I sweating in this suffocating airport, scrutinizing traveling businessmen when I could be collecting cash and dancing my ass off in a drunken state of euphoria? I suppose you'd like to know?

Well, okay, but get ready. It's a long story and I guarantee you'll hate me when it's done.

It all began about six months ago when I literally bumped into Mia during my shift at the grocery store. She was kind enough to forgive my clumsiness, which was great, because it turned out she worked there too – it was her first day. And it was just her day job; at night she was a dancer. No surprise there, she was gorgeous with penetrating brown eyes, beautiful long dark legs, and a figure that had even the straightest girls reconsidering their sexual preferences. Everyone wanted to be friends with her. I guess I was one of the lucky ones, especially considering I nearly knocked her unconscious at our first encounter.

It didn't occur to me, of course, to ask what kind of dancer she was. I just assumed it was a

2

post-economic-downturn talent-turned-hobby she liked to indulge in at the rec center. It didn't take me long to notice that the rec center paid her very well…in stacks of small bills…

"I'm a stripper in the evenings," she explained. "It pays very well. You should try it sometime. You've got the body for it."

I almost laughed in her face, but kept my composure. She could see me, bright as day. Why she thought I ought to be up on stage in front of a crowd of men was beyond me. I didn't take her up on her offer, but she knew better than to leave me alone about it.

She was more convincing than I'd expected, so much so that even before that momentous day when I shuffled shyly into the Men's Den behind her, she'd already had me convinced that this was the answer to all my problems. Nothing would have stopped me. The shoddy buildings that flanked the club didn't deter me, nor did the graffiti on the outer cement walls or the vagrants pissing in the nearby ditch (though they did inspire me to enter with an air of caution). Something about this – maybe my friendship with Mia, maybe the rebellion of it, maybe it was just the mystery, who knows – had me hooked.

It was still daylight outside when Mia threw her body into the handle of the back door, forcing it open against its will. Tendrils of smoke made a hasty exit from the dark and dank interior, but Mia blew right through without hesitation. She looked composed and confident in her brown miniskirt and crop top, while I must've looked like a scared cat with my unkempt hair, wide eyes, and khaki pants pared with an ill-fitted tank top. Fashion had never been my thing as evidenced by my college photos that featured fully buttoned shirts, ankle-length knit skirts, and one consistent pair of sneakers. Khaki pants were a daring venture for me.

3

The other dancers hadn't arrived yet so our only audience was the owner, slouched on a couch in the dressing room just inside the door, flipping through an old porn magazine while he enjoyed his cigarette.

"Randy!" Mia ordered. "Get your ass up. Your new girl is here."

He hardly flinched. Instead, he took a long draw from his cigarette, and rested his head against the couch as a few pieces of hot ash dusted his wrinkled t-shirt and baggy black jeans. He flicked them aside like would-be crumbs and held the stub out for Mia. She took it gratefully at first, enjoying her own long draw, then gave him an expectant look that would've had me on my knees begging for mercy.

He rolled his eyes and glanced back at me. "This is your girl?" he drawled, lazily.

I stood up a little straighter and sucked my belly in a little tighter.

"God, you are such an ass," Mia scolded. "Get up and get a good look at her, for fuck's sake."

Randy sported a cheeky smile. "I love it when you call me names." He slapped her ass as he stood and ambled towards me.

Wow. He was rather tall – probably six-foot-three and in decent shape. His five o'clock shadow in conjunction with the stench of cigarettes and rum on his breath indicated that first impressions weren't his number one concern, but they definitely added to his sex appeal.

I closed my eyes and let out a deep, steady breath.

"She's nervous," Randy barked. "How the fuck is she going to handle a whole crowd if she can't even sit still while I'm checking her out?"

My teeth clenched and my eyes narrowed. I glanced at Mia who just shrugged.

"I've recruited almost all of your dancers

4

for almost three years now," she countered, smugly, "You should have learned not to question me. Look at Crystal, Charlotte, Dashia…I know when I see future talent."

Randy's deep blue eyes scaled my body from head to toe, his hands stroking my skin and raising goose bumps across my arms and legs. "She certainly has the equipment…" His eyebrows tethered. "Is she even old enough for this? I don't take children; the motherfuckers who get horny off that shit know better than to come in here."

"I'm twenty-four," I announced with as much stamina as I could muster.

He grunted. "Exactly how innocent are you? A virgin?"

I flushed. "No." My voice shook and it pissed me off. I clenched my fists. "I know how to handle a man." My cheeks turned a beet red reserved only for salads and rug burns. I was mortified as I stood there like a pig on display at the state fair. I forced myself to relax and dug up my self-confidence. I rested my hand on my hip and looked Randy right in the eye – a stark reminder that he was dealing with a person, and a very stubborn one at that.

He stared back, unfazed. "Are you sure about that? Because you look like the type who still lives with Mommy and Daddy."

My blood boiled, but I kept my cool. "My parents live outside of Vegas; I live here. End of story."

He cocked an eyebrow. "And your boyfriend?"

I shrank. "I don't have one anymore. My relationships don't usually last long."

He grunted. "Good. The last thing I need is another jealous dickwad with itchy fists and no cash." He gestured around the room. "So why this? What the fuck brings a pretty little thing like you to a rat hole like this?"

5

I glanced at Mia and she nodded. With effort, I returned Randy's hardened gaze. "My parents are yuppie assholes. They cut me off the second I had sex with my college boyfriend and I need money to pay off my student loans." I paused to consider. "And frankly, telling my parents that their prudish beliefs turned their daughter into a stripper would piss them off in a very satisfying way."

"A rebellious one, eh?" He caressed his stubble with long, calloused fingers. "You sure you can handle this shit? You seem a bit soft, and I'm not talking about your well-moisturized skin."

My eyes narrowed. "Depends: Are your customers assholes too?" I held his gaze until, almost without my permission, my hand snuck up to my mouth. I placed my index finger sensually on my bottom row of teeth, and then tugged gently on my lower lip while my eyes gave his body a good, long top-to-bottom analysis. I shrugged. "Either way, you don't look like much of a challenge."

I heard Mia suppress a snicker.

Randy stood up straight, cleared his throat, and turned to Mia. "You've got ten minutes to teach her something that convinces me she can dance. I'll be in my office."

Shit. I thought I had him.

Mia hardly flinched. "Don't worry, Ellie, I know how to convince Randy of pretty much anything."

Fifteen minutes later, I was standing in the center of a dark and worn stage in nothing but my bra and panties (I really wish Mia had prepped me for that), with Mia a few inches away bedazzled in a similar manner. A single spotlight was concentrated on us, promising to reveal every zit and blemish on my skin. Randy had slunk down in an old chair on the main floor, watching with interest and just a touch of disbelief. He waved his hand, signaling us to begin.

6

As Mia strode to the back of the stage to start the music, I glanced down at myself. I was standing almost completely naked in front of a complete stranger. So odd. For a small moment, I imagined myself back on campus in a classy blouse and a pair of pristine blue jeans, my long brown hair cascading down my back. I was a straight-A student. I followed all of Mom and Dad's rules. I went to church and volunteered at the rape crisis center. I did everything perfectly. Oh, except sex. I had a lot of sex with a lot of very nerdy boys.

But in every other way, I was the perfect daughter. And now I was going to learn how to take my clothes off for horny men in exchange for fistfuls of bills and, as my mom would say, sacrifice my "inner beauty."

I had been so perfect for so long, yet so empty and torn inside. I was never a happy person, but I did my best to keep up the facade after graduation. I failed miserably. I felt like a dried up ocean, a desert with nothing to comfort me but prickly cacti and burning hot sand. I had nothing without my academic successes. And here I was, about to fall even deeper; peel that modest skirt off my hot, sweaty skin and throw it into a mass of drooling men so they could stare at the most real, most vulnerable version of me. It terrified me.

It was exhilarating.

Mia set the music to a deep and delicious hip-hop tune and strode to her pole, nodding at me to approach mine. The routine was simple: we both did a couple of sexy turns, eyeing each other the whole time. Then we came together in the middle, executing the age-old night club button popper: the girl-on-girl floor grind. It was such a menial move, I wasn't sure Randy would be impressed, but when I glanced over and saw him squirm in his seat, I knew I was in.

Mia really does know how to get straight to a man's dick.

7

I began my first set two nights later. From day one, I realized something I hadn't expected – see, at the start, this whole endeavor was about making ends meet; it was all about the money. But that first night I walked on stage, I realized something even more critical, and nothing less than absurdly shocking: I *loved* being a stripper.

Chapter 2

I still remember well the deafening music that blared in my ears and the tingles of alcoholic rapture that spread across my limbs my first night of work at the club. My face was caked in blue eye shadow, red blush, and gobs of glitter that made my skin itch. It took all my self-control to keep from scratching my own damn face off. I sported a sexy little number Mia had helped me pick out: a gold two-piece with beads cascading down the top to decorate my bare belly. Anywhere else I would have felt awkward dressed so dramatically, but at the club, I fit right in. It was like playing dress-up and getting paid for it.

Like a naïve teen flashing her first fake I.D., I fluttered my most fantastical bedroom eyes to my first potential customer: a frustratingly apathetic dickhead sitting beside me at the bar. I coughed as he released another puff of his cigarette and moaned quietly with the deep and sensual beat of the hip-hop music.

I nudged him with my elbow. "Are we working a few more shots here, baby, or have you had enough?" My flirting skills needed work but my insecurities were forced to take a reluctant back seat to the necessity of covering the rent.

Dickhead huffed. "Depends. How much you gunnin' for tonight? I haven't gotten paid yet, sweetheart."

From the corner of my eye, I could see the drooling men at the front of the room by the stage, waving their money at the bikini-clad objects of their obsession. Their efforts were soon thwarted as the girls caught sight of fresher blood: a young political up-and-comer who was standing uncomfortably at the back of the room. Within seconds, the dollar-clutching patrons were left destitute as the girls clamored towards the expensive suit and tie.

With a roll of my eyes, I turned back to Dickhead. "I may be able to work in a Friday night discount, just for you." I winked. Money was tight and I'd already shelled out fifty bones to dance there that night, but chunk change was better than no change. And anyways, "it's better than getting tangled up in that mess over there."

I glanced over to see the politician unsuccessfully trying to fend off several of my very aggressive colleagues. He looked completely lost. It was fantastically entertaining.

It wasn't five minutes earlier that the politician had sauntered through the doors of the Men's Den in his slacks, shiny cuff links, and very expensive watch, his security flanking him at a very intimate distance. His eyes scanned the room cautiously through the thick cloud of smoke, as though hoping to find some essence of familiarity. His expensive jewelry was in odd contrast to the worn wood laminate floors and neon lights that flickered off his pretty face. Politicians were certainly not an unusual sight in this particular

10

locale, but celebrities were delicacies on our menu; I knew the girls were going to be having sissy fights in no time.

I had no personal interest in getting my hair yanked and my reputation dragged through the dirt, so I continued to keep my distance and grabbed another shot at the bar with Dickhead while I watched the other girls close in on their rare prey.

Mia would get him; I was certain of that. I wasn't even sure why the other girls tried. But somehow, Lacy got there first, flirting shamelessly while I laughed raucously at the absurd scene. She looked so determined while the politician looked so goddamn awkward.

"Some guys get all the luck," Dickhead huffed.

I turned back to him, flashed a charming smile, and placed my hand on his thigh, caressing him like I'd seen the other girls do. "I'm here for you, baby, don't worry about him."

"You want another?"

I shrugged. "Whatever you want, handsome."

He raised his finger to the bartender and another shot glass of gleaming clear fluid slid in front of me.

As I raised the vodka to my lips, the sound of shattering glass echoed across the room. I craned my neck to the left just in time to see Mia smack Lacy in the face just inches from the shocked expression of the handsome politician. She pushed her over one of the bar tables, scattering a few cocktails in her wake. Lacy was back on her feet in seconds, grabbing Mia's hair and dragging her away screaming, unwittingly opening up a small wedge of space next to Richy Rich, the Political Hopeful.

I chuckled as Crystal ditched one of her regulars to dive in for her chance on the politician's

11

payroll. Bad move. The regular was pissed and wasted no time telling the flustered politician to stay the hell away from his girl. The politician took a couple of blows to the face before staggering out of the crowd towards the door.

I lost sight of him as the tables turned and Lacy found herself being dragged to the dressing room, Mia's arm hooked around her throat. I knew that was the last time I'd see her at the club.

They all say Mia's the Mamma Goose of the club – you don't fuck with her unless you want to get flattened or fired.

I returned to my shot glass, a bit taken aback by the wealth of entertainment at my disposal, but the chaos began to calm as Randy barged in with his thugs, throwing out Crystal's regular and giving the girls his special recipe of 'what for.' I was in the process of returning to my sales pitch when my eye caught sight of the politician over by the door. Apparently, his black eye wasn't enough motivation to ditch this shithole. He seemed to be arguing with his 'muscle,' that is until his eyes found mine through a small break in the crowd. He held my gaze with a look I knew all too well. I immediately turned away and glowered.

Please don't come over here; please don't come over here...

A man approached to my left.

Please don't be the politician; please don't be the politician...

"Scotch and soda, and a glass of ice for my face, please," said the polished voice.

Damnit.

The bartender gave him a dishcloth along with his order. He smoothly wrapped up the ice and placed it painstakingly upon his swollen eye. I stared straight ahead, my mind racing to find a way to bag the Dickhead to my right before the

12

politician to my left could get a chance to open his lying mouth. I wasn't quick enough.

"Bit of a dangerous place here, isn't it? How do you survive?" the politician said as he leaned so close that I could smell his high-end lobbyist-infused musk.

I responded in the most patronizing manner my innocent ovaries could concoct. "If it's too much for you, sweetie, the door is over there." I cocked one eyebrow and sucked on a slice of lime. "Anyways, I might ask the same of you and the crowd you run with." I may have been a rookie in the stripper world, but I knew how the political world functioned; if he was going to try to start a conversation, he was going to get an earful.

He turned to me. "You know who I am?"

I scowled. "Everyone knows who you are. Why do you think the vultures descended?"

He laughed. "So that doesn't happen to everyone, does it?"

I didn't really know how to answer that one so I simply rolled my eyes in lieu of saying what I really wanted to: *I don't like politicians. Ergo, I don't like you. Go away.* I stared down into my shot glass, wishing it could magically replicate into five or six more.

"So why didn't you fly on over to join the vultures?" He cocked his head to the side. "You don't like me?"

"We all have rules." I tipped back the shot, recalling Mia's lecture on setting standards and sticking to them. "'Never entertain a douchebag politician' is my first one."

His face flattened. "I can see why my colleagues don't come to this particular establishment often."

"You don't look like you get out much at all, Sugar Daddy. Is this your first time playing with girls who don't wear pencil skirts and tennis bracelets?"

13

"Well, it certainly will be my last." He gulped the rest of his drink and threw some cash on the counter, drumming his fingers against the hard wood counter as he waited for the bartender to make change.

To my relief, Dickhead finally made his move. "Okay, sweetheart, you goin' with him or me? If that body is as sharp as your tongue, I can spare ten bucks for a lap dance."

I grimaced. What cheap bullshit. I could make that in a short hour as a checker at the grocery store. I glanced around to find an excuse to escape, but my only out was the politician, an even less appealing proposition.

Dickhead stood before I could push away from the bar. "Come on, baby." He leaned into my ear. "I'll throw in an extra fiver if you show me your pussy."

I shouldn't have been insulted. I shouldn't have even been fazed. Both Mia and Randy warned me about this. Shitty lowball offers and pussy peek-a-boo requests were a daily affair in this line of business. But I still hadn't habituated myself to such degrading insult, so instead of smiling and flirting my way into a higher bid like Mia would have, I jumped to make a hasty exit. But before I could so much as pull my ass off the bar stool, Dickhead had me by the arm.

"Not so fast," he slurred, "I've got something special no other guy can offer." He dipped his other hand into his pants.

Before I could rip my arm from his grasp, the politician was at my side, shoving him against the bar counter.

"She said no, asshole. Leave her alone."

I turned on the politician like a charging bull. "Back off," I seethed, wedging myself between the two of them like a lame ass peewee football referee. "I don't need you standing up for me like

14

one of your cheap escorts. I can handle my own shit."

The politician glowered and stepped backwards.

I turned to Dickhead, readjusting my top and contemplating my next move. I shored up my insecurities and repeated the exact phrase I'd heard Crystal say earlier that evening. "Fifteen bucks, no pussy, and keep your goddamn hands to yourself."

He nodded with a sick smile.

"No, fuck that," the politician cried defensively.

I could barely make out the look of derision on his face amidst the smog and glaring lights.

"You don't have to do that. I'll pay you five-hundred dollars to get out of here and go somewhere nice with me."

It should have been a tempting offer, but the insinuation behind his words caused rage to explode across my face. "I'm not a whore, fucker." I gave him my most menacing glare. "The hustlers that sell out to you and your bribing friends hang out on the Strip." I turned to back to Dickhead. "Let's go. There's a private room over by the stage."

I grabbed his hand and stormed off. I chanced a glance backwards, delighting in the look of utter insult and failure on the face of the politician. Though not the ideal first night as a stripper, at least I'd accomplished something: I'd always wanted to leave a man speechless.

The sullen politician's face, the heavy beat, and the shining lights fade from my imagination and the reality of the crowded, arid, white-walled airport comes disappointingly back into view.

Remember that goddamn wooden bench I mentioned earlier? My ass is still glued to it. It's admittedly not a great perch for musing, but my memories of that first night as a dancer just six months ago are all too vivid as people hustle and

15

bustle through the airport with all the energy of the strip club and not a hint of the pizzazz.

I wish I were stripping right now. At least it would keep me busy. Shitty airport peanuts, drinking fountain water, and the cold sting of potential rejection are just not the cascade of roses I had imagined them to be. A few people who arrived here after me have already boarded and taken off on their planes – a shitty reminder that I'm still here, still alone, and still potentially insane.

A lovey dovey couple walks by pulling matched luggage and a designer handbag behind them as they canoodle with no regard for the passengers around them. I think I'm gonna barf. Of course, I'd love it if I were on the receiving end of that kind of affection. But circumstances being what they are, I fucking hate them.

You know, we'd better wait until I have a cold hard drink in my hand to swim any further down that rat hole. Let's get back to the story; it's a lovely distraction.

Chapter 3

Up until my official acceptance into the world of exotic dancing (yes, I like to make it sound way cooler than it is, thank you very much), both Mia and I had been bagging groceries for minimum wage. I was a recent college grad with an English degree – hooray for the unemployed class of 2014 – but the writer's market was more disappointing than my ex-boyfriend's willy so I was doing what was required to get by.

Luckily, a few weeks after Mia convinced me to join her at her unusual but lucrative side gig, I was able to quit my job at the grocery store so I could work on my dancing during the day. I'd always been ambitious, and I wanted to be the best, highest paid stripper at the Men's Den.

After several months, I had improved a lot. I wasn't quite there yet, but I was getting more and more popular all the time. Unfortunately, popularity had its downsides.

One of those nights, about two or three months into my new career, things had started out great enough. My g-string was stuffed with twenties – a rare occasion – and I was enjoying the hooting and hollering as I wrapped my stiletto around the stage pole and swooped into a new move I'd mastered the week before. I was hot, and being hot in a strip club full of randy, sometimes wealthy, and sometimes gorgeous men is *great*.

Unless one of *them* walks in.

Here's the thing: I'd gotten used to the diversity of the clientele at the club. Some men were needy, some standoffish and others very vocal. Some were fat, some were skinny, some were hot (we'd fight like bridesmaids competing for the Bridal bouquet when they walked in), but let's face it: there weren't many being drafted as male models. But for the most part, they were kind and respectful and held a deep admiration for the female form that typically kept their behavior in line. I got used to enjoying the admiring eyes of even the most unattractive men – an essential skill for any woman giving a lap dance to a complete stranger.

And then there were the "Pots" as we called them. Ugh. Dancing for them was like unclogging a toilet: no one enjoyed it but someone had to do it. They weren't necessarily called Pots because they were physically unappealing – we enjoyed dancing for plenty of men who weren't attractive – it was more a matter of persona: the glint of greed in their eyes, the way they leered at us while simultaneously licking their lips as if readying themselves for a well-deserved meal. They were scumbags and normally we'd run the other way, but we had a job to do and as long as they didn't break the rules, the boss couldn't kick them out.

The Pot that walked in on this particular night was, well, large, and not in the good places. The rolls that cascaded down his body were accented by glints of hot sweat that trailed from his thick and stocky neck. The other dancers knew him

18

well as the "asshole that loves ass holes." I'm not sure I want to know how he got this nickname, but I imagine it had something do with the resident whore, Priscilla.

I'd been there three months that fateful day he walked in. I had managed to use my amateur status to avoid patronizing most of the Pots, but my time had run out and the girls were all too happy to pawn him off on me. At least they were kind enough to grant me looks of pity in their wake.

"Ellie," hissed a voice. It was Mia.

I glared. "What?"

"The first time is always the worst, but it gets better after that. Just close your eyes and pretend he's Brad Pitt. If you concentrate really hard, it doesn't seem so bad."

My anxiety elevated. Her words were a stark reminder of how much I didn't want to do this.

Mia took my hand tenderly and handed me off to the Pot in a regretful fashion. My eyes plead with her, but she conveniently had to run off to handle some other priority.

"Hey baby," the Pot said, his eyes aglow with lust. I forced myself to look him in the eye. Much to my surprise, he staggered for a moment, taken aback. His expression quickly changed to curiosity with just a hint of fear. He raised his hand to my right cheek.

I smacked it down with fervor. "Here's the rules: I can handle a little touching, but my boobs, pussy, and my face are off limits, understand?"

He laughed, a deep, guttural laugh. "I see you're still a feisty little one. "

I'm *still* feisty? My memory wasn't great, but I felt pretty damn certain I'd never danced for him before. I forced a pleasant smile. "You've got me confused with one of the other girls."

He shrugged. "Maybe I do, maybe I don't.

19

Either way, I bet you've been waiting on that luscious ass all day for a guy like me."

My stomach felt queasy. And what's more, he seemed to like it. Yuck. I swallowed and closed my eyes, drumming up images of Brad Pitt while feigning a smile.

I can do this. Yeah, I can. As long as he doesn't–

"I think I'd like a special treat tonight, Miss Titty. Show me to the Mud Room."

Ah, fuck.

The blood drained from my face. I considered running, running away and never coming back. Something about this man made me very, very uncomfortable. I was sure I could get my job at the grocery store back. I certainly wouldn't be called "Miss Titty" there. But remember what I mentioned before about being ambitious? Well, as sickening as it was, I didn't want to be weak. I had committed to this career and, damnit, I was going to kick ass at it.

I gingerly took his hand and led him to the semi-private room at the back of the club. It was hidden behind a faux door, reserved for those with serious stacks of cash. I comforted myself with thoughts of hundred-dollar bills, new shoes, and a real meal at a real restaurant once my Mud Room torture was over.

Ah, the Mud Room. The place strippers love to hate. It's better than getting felt up in a back alley, but only if you're in the right mood.

It wasn't my first time dancing for someone in the Mud Room, just my first time with a Pot. My first experience in the Mud Room had been just two weeks earlier. Before that night, the entire room scared the living hell out of me – dusky and dank, with rough cement walls and not a single window. Just two light bulbs swung dangerously from the moldy, dripping roof, their small glow carving out the edges of the indistinct human shadows huddling in their chairs. I had the impression it

20

was once an oversized walk-in closet, and that the club had every intention of continuing to make it appear as such from the outside. Its isolated location meant that every puff of smoke and every drip of perspiration remained infinitesimally carved into the stuffy ambience. Even from the hallway just outside the door, the smell of sweat, whiskey, and cum infiltrated the senses.

I got lucky – the first guy who took me in there was hot as all hell. I'd only manage to nab him because Mia threatened to beat the living shit out of any girls who even considered taking a crack at him. Always my protector, she wanted my first Mud Room dance to be as pleasant as possible.

He led me by the hand to the door that held the crooked sign reading "Equipment". The bulge beneath his jeans gave away his excitement for our little rendezvous and I couldn't hide that I, too, was eager. He fought with the rickety doorknob and finally kicked the base with his heel to force it open. He pulled me into the murky room, the low and smooth porn music and soft moans of male satisfaction immediately filling my ears. I grabbed a cigar from the box by the door and offered it to him.

"No, baby, all I want is you," he whispered.

He sat down and I stepped back nervously, knowing what I had to do. I could hear a couple of the other girls coming around me, their clients groaning with pleasure. I'd be lying if I said the sound wasn't erotic music to my ears.

I leaned into my handsome customer so my lips were just off his ear. "You know the rules, hon. I'll do anything you ask me to and take off anything you want at your command, except my thong. This is the only room where you can touch me wherever and whenever you want, but I'm not allowed to touch you…" I lowered my voice to a more seductive tone, "…even if you beg me. If you're good and you follow the rules, I'll come so

21

hard you'll never be satisfied by another woman again." Mia had given me that script. I'd practiced it for weeks knowing I'd eventually have to face the music.

The man took a deep breath and released it slowly, placing his hands on my hips and licking my belly button. His tongue ring tickled and I giggled.

"Dance for me, baby," he breathed.

The experience was hotter than I could ever have imagined. Within minutes, I was sitting on his lap, my top crumpled nearby on the floor, his hands exploring everything from the neck down. I didn't even have to fake an orgasm.

I ended up going home with him later that night; our chemistry was far too amazing not to take a chance on a post-work encounter. We giggled and fucked all night long in his tiny apartment near the airport. He asked me to stay through the next day so we could hit the strip together before my next shift. The night exceeded all expectations, but when morning rolled around and the sun touched the edges of his pale pink butt cheeks, I knew I'd do what I always did: I grabbed my things and snuck out.

I know. The guy is the one who's supposed to do that. But for some reason I've never been able to stomach being with someone longer than one night. Something about it feels terrifying and, well, suffocating.

But that's another story. The Pot's hand in mine, once again, off to the Mud Room I went, but this time without a hint of hopeful anticipation. He shoved the door open, copping a feel of my ass as I walked by, and found a chair near the end of a row of about five men, all caught up in the ecstasy of the dimly lit room.

The Pot sat down, his eyes scaling my body inch by inch. He reached out his enormous hand and delicately touched my purple miniskirt,

22

flipping the sequined ties between his fingers. I begrudgingly swirled my hips around, moving in and out of his waiting palm, and twisted my fingers nervously in my hair as I begrudgingly listened for my next instructions.

"Turn around," he commanded.

I'm sorry, what? You hate women?

I held my tongue. My eyes shut tight, I found my image of Brad Pitt naked on the beach, and complied.

*　　　*　　　*　　　*　　　*

The experience could have been worse. At least that's what I tried to convince myself as the stale odor of the Pot made my stomach churn. I reminded myself that I was alive, I got through the awful "first time" with a Pot, and I knew I'd be okay in a few hours. But the moment I left that room – the smiling scumbag sliding several hundred-dollar bills in my top and stealing a twist of my nipple – I couldn't get to the dressing room fast enough. I did my best not to run through the club, but I had to get out. I was suffocating. I burst through the dressing room door, kicked off my stilettos and collapsed in tears next to the trash. I didn't usually imbibe myself in the act of crying, but I couldn't get the image of his leering eyes out of my head. And in this case, the crying helped. A lot, actually. I opened a window and sank depleted to the floor by the mirror, waiting for the awful images of his sausage-like hands on me to dissipate.

You've been here before, Ellie. The same thing happened when you gave a Pot a Lap dance for the first time. You'll be okay.

My breathing was starting to return to normal when Randy came crashing through the door. "What the fuck do you think you're doing?" he cried.

23

His blue eyes were boring into me like a couple of rusty screwdrivers. In my delirium, I was tempted to let myself get lost in them, but I felt a bit lightheaded and couldn't do much more than stare in confusion.

"You practically sprinted away from him!" he continued. "Look at you. Your fucking top is bleeding hundred dollar bills. Is that not enough for you? Do you want him to think you find him repulsive?"

He was pretty irate, his face a bright tomato-ey red that reminded me of my mother's garden growing up. I looked down at the floor, my mind spinning. I didn't know what to say.

Mia walked in and saved the day. "Randy, give her a fucking break."

I snapped back to reality. Her comfort with confrontation always impressed me.

"It was her first time. You remember the first time I had to give a Pot the special? I was in worse shape than her."

Randy ran his hand through his chin-length hair, reluctantly considering her argument but clearly still reeling from my display of disaffection. "Just...take care of her, ok? Get her cleaned up. You're both up in ten minutes." He turned to the door and slammed his hand hard against the frame. "Fucking whores," he spat. And then he was gone.

Mia walked me to the couch, gave me a slice of stale pizza and a glass of water, and dabbed my forehead with a cool damp paper towel.

"He's a real dick sometimes," Mia coddled. "He doesn't know what it's like."

"I'm just glad you were here," I murmured. "You're the only one he listens to."

Mia's face flushed as she tried to suppress a shy smile.

There had to be something going on between those two. I'd sensed it for a while, but

24

this moment confirmed it. Mia had encountered some pretty embarrassing moments since I'd met her, but I'd never once seen her blush. I cocked an eyebrow hoping to get some details, but she sneered and stomped off to her locker to get ready for the next number.

I pulled myself up from the liquor-stained couch and stumbled to the mini fridge for a Diet Coke. I popped a Tylenol and let the brown gurgling liquid sooth my throat. I felt better, maybe even a little proud.

I did it. I made it through one of the shittiest experiences imaginable.

I started to feel whole again, recovery coming much quicker than I expected. I reached into my locker next to Mia's and pulled out my black-feathered two-piece to prepare for the group number. This particular costume was one of my sexiest outfits. I always felt like a million bucks in it. As the fog from the Pot began to dissipate, my normal apprehension and excitement about going back on stage started to seep back in.

God, it thrilled me to be up there, flooded with colored lights, moving smoothly to a captivated, adoring crowd. No one noticed a single weakness when I was up there. It was as if I lived as a perfect and unblemished version of myself every night. The cheers and the screams were like blood to me. I barely noticed the cash thrown at me and tucked into my g-string; it was the worship I was there for.

Of course, it wasn't all ego boosts and smiles. Outside of the obvious run-ins with the very unappealing Pots, occasionally we'd also get a lonely guy in the crowd who would wait after hours to try to catch us on our way home. That was always awkward. The first time one of them approached me with a bouquet of flowers, I tried to explain to him that what we did was an act, that the looks we shared and the eye candy I provided

25

was just part of the show. I learned very quickly that this didn't work. It only took one stalker to stage a kidnapping outside the club for me to realize I couldn't give these guys the time of day anymore.

God, it's dangerous to be beautiful.

Hahaha! Did I seriously just think that? Ah man, this place is already beginning to make me crazy. I'm gonna lose you before we even get to the good part.

I look at my watch: six-thirty in the evening. Where is he? Am I in the right place? Is this the right bench? It would totally be my luck to get stuck waiting here for hours for some guy who doesn't have the balls to show up. But he isn't like that...is he?

I'm probably confusing you. Don't worry; it will all make sense later. It looks like I may have all night so let's get back to the story. I was waiting to go on stage...

Well, 'stage' may be a strong word in this context. Our club made good money but it's not like we had the funds of the clubs on the Strip. The 'stage' was more of a slightly elevated platform. It had four poles and decent lighting, but it was covered in laminate flooring. I was quite sure most of our clientele didn't know the difference, but I'm not ashamed to admit that I often closed my eyes and imagined I was dancing on real hardwood. The kind that makes that satisfying *click-clack* sound under your heels.

Someday, maybe.

But so it was. Adorned in my killer two-piece, I followed my fellow dancers out on stage, carrying myself with a swagger that appeared completely unaware of the hell I went through just minutes before.

That night, I was one with the pole.

26

Chapter 4

As was standard protocol, we began the evening with introductions. During the first few months of my employment, I hated this part. It didn't take long to realize that this wasn't standard practice for most clubs, nor were our regular group performances. We did it as some kind of weird throwback to Randy's musical theatre days.

I know: Randy in musical theatre? I've always been afraid to ask more questions about that.

Either way, from day one I felt awkward on stage and never got the kind of applause the other girls received. It was embarrassing, and I'm actually quite surprised I didn't get fired; I was a pretty awful dancer at first. Mia must have had something to do with my continuous employment. But by now I was far more steady on my feet and had improved enough that I typically enjoyed a very enthusiastic response.

"Gentleman, let's meet one of your top dolls: the sexy and ravishing Nevaeh!"

I know, I know, it doesn't get any cheesier than "heaven" spelled backwards. But hey, it was original, and I'm quite certain it earned me an extra two hundred bucks a night. I mean, what man doesn't secretly hope there are strip teases in heaven?

I sauntered out on stage as the blinding lights made my sequined outfit sparkle like diamonds. Hoots and hollers rose up from the crowd and fists of cash were tossed on stage and tucked into my g-string before I even got started. I began at the pole with a Frodo, then slid into an Extended Frodo (no, I'm not talking Hobbits here; use Google, for Chrissake). It was my signature move and typically worth a few whoops and screams; this night was no exception. I continued my short routine, finishing with an erotic waist bend. I ran my finger up my leg, dramatically flipped my hair, and crossed my hands across my chest and then into my hair as I swayed off to the side of the stage. Mia was always after me and she was by far the most popular. As she took her place on stage – every man in the room sitting forward in his seat, eyes glued – I relaxed for a moment and leaned my hand against the wall.

I scanned the crowd for potential lap dance targets and was surprised to find that not every man in the room was watching Mia. There was one man scrunched into the corner of a dark booth towards the back of the crowd who appeared to be looking…at me?

"Ellie, I think someone likes you."

One of the girls had joined me, nodding toward the same man whose eyes peeked out from below his baseball cap. I couldn't see much other than those eyes. The hat cleverly shrouded his face and the dark room shaded most of his body. I couldn't stop staring back at him. There was something about those eyes. Was it the desire in them? Were they just incredibly gorgeous? I wasn't

28

sure, but they had an effect on my entire body that sent chills from the very tips of the hairs on my head all the way down to my toes. His hand reached briefly into the light to grasp his beer.

Oh God, not the hands. Hands are like a mating call to me. Every man I've ever dated had amazing hands.

This mysterious stranger stroked his beer gently with long and confident fingers, the tendons and veins beneath his skin asserting themselves as evidence of his muscular form.

Well, that's how I imagined it, anyways.

I shuddered unexpectedly. *Ellie, be careful, you're still on stage*, I reminded myself.

I looked around to verify that there was no one else watching me. Nope; with Mia in the spotlight, I was on my own. My eyes wandered back to his and, upon closer scrutiny, I could swear he was smirking at me. Was he teasing me?

"Ellie, snap out of it!" It was Mia. She had approached to pull me back on stage for the group number.

Oh, I was ready.

I sashayed out there with the confidence of a woman who just eye-fucked Tom Hardy. I threw myself into the dance while those deep and probing eyes haunted my subconscious. Whoever he was, he was watching, and I was going to give him one hell of a show.

Each dancer split off two-by-two. I was with Candy (every strip club has to have one, right?) and I pulled her close, grinding into her leg while one hand pulled at her hair. I slid my other hand serendipitously down my side, across my flat belly, and landed softly onto the ties hanging at her hip. She threw her head back at my touch and I followed her lead, leaning my face in near her breasts and licking my lips sensually.

The men (and women, actually) went wild. A proud smile spread across Candy's face. She was

29

fairly new and had not received this kind of response before.

Oh, we're not done yet, honey. Wait until you see what I have in store for you.

In coordination with the routine, we stood back-to-back, body-rolled to the floor, then grasped hands, slowly rising back up to stand. I turned to face her back, swept her hair behind her neck, and breathed softly onto her skin. My hands clung daintily to the front of her hips and we pulsated backwards in circles to the music, the other girls in perfect time with us. I caressed her gorgeous skin slowly and carnally with my perfectly adorned nails until I reached the clasp of her top. I pulled at the strings and sent her cover spiraling to the ground, her engorged breasts shining in the spotlight to cheers from our heated patrons. I was ad-libbing a little; it was encouraged for this routine. A few of the other girls grinned in surprise, then followed my example, much to the pleasure of our audience.

We returned back-to-back again, completing another lascivious body roll. My hands crept up towards my neck, a look of coy innocence on my face, and I unhooked my own top, which fell to my waist. I swear I could smell the drool emanating from the anxious spectators. I ran my hands down my side, reached behind my back, and released the remainder of my top.

After one more intense body roll, Candy and I turned to face each other again. I stole a glimpse at the crowd, hoping to catch sight of my secret admirer, but I couldn't see past the floodlights. God, I hoped he was still there.

It was all for his benefit. I imagined those haunting eyes still burrowed into me with seething pleasure. I imagined he was hard and squirming, barely able to hold himself back from running up here to throw me against the wall and ravish me. I pushed up against Candy even harder than I had

30

before. She responded in kind and our nipples danced against each other, stimulating us to explore each other with even greater fervor.

I could feel my own wetness peaking with each move. I was dying to slip my fingers beneath the fabric of my thong to satisfy my ache. Instead I continued the libidinous molestation of my willing partner, the cheers of the crowd barely audible while the thump of my rapidly pumping blood pounded in my ears.

The dance finished and we sauntered off the stage, the girls all smiles over the incredible response from our very enthusiastic crowd. I immediately stole into the dressing room, locked the door, and flattened my back against the wall. My fingers reached straight for my burning and aching clit. I began my self-assault with deep circular motions, the intensity rising quickly as images of me straddled across my new lover infected my imagination.

I came hard, the fingers of my other hand sliding in and out of me with reckless abandon. It took every measure of self-control to avoid crying out. Not that it mattered; it wasn't unusual for us ladies to satisfy our needs back here – sometimes together, sometimes alone – but I wanted this moment to be private. I didn't want anyone else to see my vulnerability.

I sank to the floor, endorphins racing, satisfaction achieved at long last. I closed my eyes and considered falling asleep in that very spot, but I resisted. Lap dances were next on the menu, and I was likely to be in high demand after that steamy number.

My eyes shot open. *Will he want a lap dance?*

I sat up straight, my energy replenished, and rushed back out to the platform with a hopeful heart.

*   *   *   *   *

31

He was gone. *Goddamnit.*

When did he leave? Did he even see my titillating exhibition? Oh my God, what if I looked like a total idiot up there, dancing my brains out for some guy who wasn't even watching?

No. I knew I didn't look stupid. The applause that still rang in my ears confirmed that.

Ok, pause: I've got to stretch my legs. Even stupendously important wooden airport benches aren't meant to be occupied by girls waiting for mysterious and potentially nonexistent boyfriends.

As I turn to pick up my purse, I feel someone approach me from behind. My legs stiffen and my hands numb. Shit, is this it? Is he finally here? I turn slowly, fingers shaking, terrified of what I might see.

But it isn't him. Of course not, that would be too easy. It's a janitor, gesturing toward my empty cardboard coffee cup and asking if I've finished. I hand it to him with a grimace, wishing he really was my mystery man. He's not bad looking. And hell, I'd take anyone right now just to know I didn't dream this whole thing up.

I pop over to the concourse cafe for another coffee and feel a little better after I've flirted with the barista.

It's now seven o'clock. He did say the flight leaves at eight thirty-five. I mean, my understanding has always been that it's vitally important to be two hours early for any flight, but maybe he has one of those fancy security passes.

Or maybe he has a private jet! I imagine myself walking across the tarmac in the sights of hundreds of passengers, all wishing they were the one approaching the shiny miniature plane of a handsome billionaire. I laugh to myself. I've always had such an active imagination. Plan for the worst, Ellie: boils, a bald spot, and a missing eye. Yeah, I'll be ready for that.

32

Of course I know none of that is the case. 'How?', you ask? Well I'm not going to tell you that right now. It'll ruin the rest of the story. And if he really does have a private jet, I've got another hour and half to kill!

Let's get back to the club before you bombard me with any more questions.

Did I mention he wasn't there when I returned anxiously to the floor to give him a lap dance? Well, he wasn't, the bastard.

My disappointment was palpable but palatable. The rest of the evening at the club passed as usual, boring and lackluster, my momentary spark of excitement and mystery doused, and my professionalism stretching to pick up the slack. The problem with moments of elation is the striking emptiness left in their wake.

I had almost made it through the entire night without incident when I stumbled into the dressing room on one of my breaks to find Mia strangling one of the other girls against the wall. I freaked out, ran over and pulled Mia off her – no easy task.

The girl skitted away, and I turned to Mia. "What the fuck was that all about?"

She gave me a look that told me to leave her alone about it, but something wasn't right. There was rage in her eyes, but also a touch of...pity?

And suddenly I knew what it was. "Mia," I warned.

She shook her head. "I took care of it, Ellie."

"I don't need your fucking pity. How long have you been doing this? Have you all been talking about me behind my back?"

"I'm protecting you, Ellie. These girls can be brutal. Trust me, you need me."

"No, I don't!" I slammed my fist against the wall in frustration. "Jesus. You didn't need to choke her, you know."

Mia shrugged. "She deserved it."

33

"I can handle myself, Mia. And I can handle what anyone else has to say about the shit hand I've been dealt."

"No you can't, goddamnit! You can barely come to grips with it yourself. When I catch the other girls gossiping about it, I take care of it. End of story."

She walked out before I could protest any longer. I felt wounded; lost. The one thing I had always hated most – the stares and the whispers – had now seeped into my life here, too. I couldn't live this way again. I needed just a hint of peace amongst the oppressive drama that leaked from every crevice of this place. I had enough conflict at home…

I shut the thoughts from my mind and stormed back onto the floor, fists clenched.

When I finally returned home that evening, I was exhausted and morose. It was Friday night so it was near three in the morning when I turned the corner onto Ponderosa Avenue and pulled into my driveway. The lights were out in the neighboring town homes, which left the sidewalk calm and quiet.

That's right, bitches, I lived in the fucking burbs. You weren't expecting that, were you? I told you I'd be the best in the business, and that means I make some damn good money; more than some of my judgmental neighbors.

Ok, I'm sorry, I'm sorry. I know you don't judge me that way. You're such a sweetheart. I wish I had neighbors so understanding. Of course…they all think I'm a bartender. I mean, come on, admit it: you wouldn't let your kids play in the yard next door to a stripper. It's practically akin to living next to a pedophile.

Sigh. Sorry. I don't like the assumptions people make about my career choices. I've got to do a better job at accepting them. There are some things in society you can't change. So rather than

34

fighting for something that will never happen, or crying about it behind closed doors, I should play the game along with everyone else and just let the world be what it is.

And anyways, when it gets to be too much, that's when I write. I write about unexpected heroes and conquering underdogs. It's a bit cliché, but to mix it up, I like to give my characters unusual hurdles, ones that might be considered sinful or harrowing to the layman. My protagonists are murderers, prostitutes, and thieves. They do horrible things to supposedly 'good' people. It makes me feel better. It reminds me the world isn't always what it seems.

Anyways, I stopped on my way inside my house to sniff the sweet aroma of the poinsettias by the driveway as I always did. I unlocked the door and dragged myself lazily up the carpeted stairs, falling asleep just before my head hit the mattress.

Chapter 5

My eyes mawed open around noon. I loved waking up at noon. My townhome was angled just right so the sun projected slivers of light through my blinds and onto the edges of my bed. Something about it was so...cozy. I didn't move a muscle, but enjoyed the feel of my body gulped into the mattress like a vat of mashed potatoes while the rays warmed my arms. That comforting sense of peace after a good night's rest washed over me. I could have laid there forever.

And I considered it. But around twelve-thirty, I started to get restless. I hopped off the bed and ran to the shower for my morning meditation.

I decided on scrambled eggs and toast for 'breakfast', and then sat myself judiciously at my desk in the front room, my notes organized, and my laptop awaiting the gentle strokes of my fingers. I opened the screen and navigated to a file called "A Ringer's Folly." After a quick scan of my last few paragraphs of work, I took a deep breath, closed my eyes, and let my mind and my emotions

36

combust together, whirling and embracing to create an infinite number of colloquial combinations. And then I waited. I waited for the perfect intersection of words, emotion, and style. My fingers began to move:

The darkness fell upon her like the stale breath of an old enemy. Her hands clasped fervently the cold hard fingers of his left hand and she squeezed in desperation, willing him to move. The light from the street lamp reflected off the shiny gold finish of his wedding ring. The ache and panic in the pits of her belly rose quickly, screaming at her – commanding her – to take action. Her tears decorated his skin as the body began to stiffen.

She didn't have much time.

She reached into her purse, pulling free a set of green wire cutters. A few dried red stains remained splattered on the old and worn tool. She always eyed the wire cutters fondly when this moment came; the most difficult and the most rewarding act of her assault. It always filled her with the deepest regret followed by feelings of closeness and acceptance she didn't know in any other context.

She aimed the small tool around his ring finger, closed her eyes, and braced herself for the sound of snapping bone – a chink that always nauseated her. She wrapped her prize fondly in a handmade handkerchief and tucked it lovingly into her bag with the wire cutters. She sat a few minutes longer, feeling the growing absence of the warmth in his skin. She imagined it filling her, energizing her, embracing her. When there was no life left to inhale, she stole quietly around the alley corner and disappeared inconspicuously into the winter snow.

My hands wouldn't stop for hours. My muse was like a well-oiled machine, pulling fuel from the depths of my soul, siphoning it through the core of my body, and splattering it haphazardly across the screen of my computer. It felt sensual,

37

maybe even spiritual, like conducting electricity. It was the only time I felt more alive than I did on stage. It was the only time it felt like the world aligned perfectly with my body and soul to give me strength and purpose.

It was almost five o'clock when my creative goddess finally dropped to her knees and surrendered for the evening. She had worked so hard; she deserved a break. And a meal! I hadn't noticed how hungry I was. I dashed to the fridge and pulled out bread, lunchmeat, mustard, and pickles for a decadent sandwich.

I couldn't believe I'd almost forgotten to eat again. I'd made that mistake one time before work and paid dearly when I got dizzy and fell into one of the tables at the club, smacking my head on the edge and packing a huge bruise that kept me out of work for three days. The incident was in my amateur days so Randy had almost thrown me out entirely. Once again, I was reminded how lucky I was to have Mia.

I flipped on the TV for a little post-meal news. More in politics – our elections were coming up and the arguments and debates were in full swing. I had built a particularly strong hatred for two political potentials who were far more popular than I would have liked. One was a republican, Smith Anderson, who fought for all those conservative social values I despised, and the other was a democrat, Brady Boswell, who came from one of those long familial lines of political power that stretched back generations. He was always touting arguments about gun control and bailouts, blah, blah, blah. As much as I wanted to support gun control, I worked with a pack of ladies – some of which had shady backgrounds – who all walked into dangerous situations on a daily basis. Few of us didn't have a concealed weapons permit; it came with the job.

My brain was starting to melt from all the

38

political ridiculousness so I switched to a music channel, wiling away my final hour before work watching the amazing Paul Patson strum away at his guitar, crooning phrases that could only be penned by a poet. Now there's a man I wouldn't mind getting my hands *and* brain into.

My soul full from the captivity of my novel and my body nourished, I headed off to work around eight. I waved to the boys playing in the street as I pulled out, wondering if I'd have one of those of my own someday. They smiled politely, if impatiently, anxious to return to their game. They were still young enough to take full advantage of every moment at their disposal and I found myself hoping I hadn't lost that childlike innocence completely. As much as I enjoyed my job, I had a very love/hate relationship with my life, one I wasn't always so sure how to manage. I ached for the singular focus of a child who never had to consider anything outside of right now.

*   *   *   *   *

Most of the girls were already in the dressing room getting ready when I arrived in a daze that was quickly shattered by the gaggle of unique and rambunctious ladies laughing and rushing around to get ready. Despite the daily drama of work, after an afternoon of TV political torture, it was a welcome escape. If I had to see the face of Smith Anderson one more time I was going to yack.

Of course, and perhaps ironically, I couldn't escape politics at work either. I walked to my locker to find a few girls gabbing on about abortion in the dressing room. Candy and Priscilla were having a riveting and rather divisive conversation.

"I just think it's up to girls to be responsible and not get fucked up," Candy said. "And if you do, then woman up. We shouldn't be able to just

39

abort a baby whenever the hell we want to."

"Where do you get the idea that women just stop off for an abortion on the way to the fucking nail salon?" Priscilla countered. "Abortions suck, but they don't kill children. They just stop them before they start."

"According to who?"

"According to the chick who got knocked up," Priscilla continued, "Her body, her decision."

They continued on for a few more minutes while I put my things in my locker. I finally couldn't stand listening to them bark at each other with lame arguments anymore. "Guys, come on, this a huge and shitty issue. Do we have to talk about it at work?

Priscilla glowered. "Oh, come on, Ellie. You're the one who always has an opinion. Why don't you tell Candy where to shove hers?"

I bit my lip. I hated arguing and I definitely didn't want to make this situation worse. But... "Nobody really knows the answer to this one, okay? Maybe if we were more thorough and mature about sex, it wouldn't be such a huge fucking problem. At the same time," I glanced at Candy, "why shouldn't we take a second to worry that we might fuck things up even more if we don't take care of a shotgun pregnancy?"

They both looked at me annoyed.

Candy raised her eyebrows. "So what, some random girl who was dumb enough to get preggo should be able to decide if her baby should die or not?"

"Well, who do you trust more? A politician? A lawyer? A doctor that the girl doesn't even fucking know?" I looked at her inquisitively.

She huffed and looked away.

"Oh come on," Priscilla stood. "Don't try to play goodie-goodie middle road, Ellie. You either let women control their own bodies or you don't. I get so tired of this bullshit."

40

Candy smirked, "I'm sure your abortion doctor does too…"

Uh oh.

Priscilla raged. "You really wanna go there, little bitch?" She stepped up to Candy, towering over her. "Why don't you take your little pussy-ass opinion back home to your little shit kid? Your fuck-ugly face never makes any money here anyways."

And that was all it took. Little Candy launched at her, fists flying. She was a hell of lot stronger than I thought. The two girls tumbled over the back of the couch, taking me down with them. My head was buried underneath Candy's elbow, slamming my right cheek against the floor. Priscilla held Candy down, hands wrapped around her neck, eyes wide with hatred. I shoved Candy's arm out of the way and dove for Priscilla's hands, attempting to pry them off but they were clenched like a vice. Luckily, Mia had overheard the scuffle and came charging in, ripping Priscilla off Candy and throwing her up against the back door.

"That is the last time you fuck with one of my girls." Mia's nose was centimeters from Priscilla's.

Priscilla hardly flinched. "You think you run this place? Which one is your new baby, the whiny little shit, or Frankenstein over there?"

My face flushed and I held my breath, images of Mia's strangling grip from the other day playing through my head on repeat. This wasn't going to end well.

Mia smacked her hard across the face leaving a deep red welt. "Out. Now."

Priscilla moved as if to retrieve her things but Mia blocked her way. She shook her head, then reached her hand out behind her. Candy responded instinctively, grabbing Priscilla's purse from the couch and placing it in her hand.

"This is all you need. That slutty little outfit

ought to be appropriate for all your bus stop clients." Mia placed her hands on her hips, the purse dangling mockingly from her index finger as she looked at Priscilla expectantly. She wasn't joking around.

Priscilla glared, surveyed her slack-jawed audience, then grabbed her purse and left.

I stared in amazement. She was wearing nothing but a very skimpy top and her g-string. Were they really going to let her go home like that?

Mia stepped away from the door and laughed. "That bitch deserves it. I should follow her and take a video. I bet it'd go viral."

Candy smiled. "Thanks, Mia."

Mia glowered. "Get the fuck back out on the floor. I'm tired of cleaning up after you."

Candy scampered off with her tail between her legs.

Mia turned to me. "Ignore Priscilla. Nobody cares, she's just trying to twist your nipple."

I raised my hand to my right cheek, scratched and swollen from my collision with the floor.

Mia pulled my hand away and regarded me sternly. "Quit it. It doesn't matter. It isn't who you are."

I nodded.

"And seriously, don't get tied up in this shit again. Sometimes it's better to just keep your mouth shut around here. I won't always be around to save you."

I opened my mouth to explain that I had nothing to do with it, but she was already on her way out. She returned to the floor and I headed to the bathroom to get cleaned up.

From there, the evening was as energetic and sweaty as ever. We began with our group number after which I took a shift waiting tables and pouring cocktails. Aside from the usual catfight between Crystal and Genevieve over a

42

regular who definitely didn't deserve to have two girls pulling each other's hair out over him, everyone seemed to be in a pretty positive mood. During my break, I popped a piece of gum and sipped a cool glass of water, trying to ignore the smell of cigarette smoke wafting in through the crack in the back door. That was Crystal – she smoked enough to give ten people cancer yet there she stood, alive, and regularly working her cardio like an Olympic gymnast.

Some people get all the good genes.

I closed my eyes for a few minutes, my body sinking slowly into the couch, reveling in the relaxation I knew would be short-lived.

"Ellie! Ellie!" My eyes flew open to a bouncy and ecstatic Candy galloping towards me with a goofy grin on her face.

"What? What?" I asked, surprised and more than a little irritated. What was her deal? She knew how much we valued our breaks.

I swiftly sat up as an idea invaded my repose. "Oh my god, there's a celebrity here, isn't there? Who is it? Where? I get dibs this time, Mia stole the last one!"

I was ready to barrel right over Candy but she stopped me.

"No!" she cried, exasperated as she attempted to keep me in place. "There's no celebrity! But it's almost as good." A sheepish grin crept across her face.

My face scrunched. What on earth was she talking about? What else could possibly be worth interrupting my rest?

"It's your boyfriend," she drawled wryly. "He's here".

The confusion on my face persisted. She'd gone mad; everyone knew I didn't have a boyfriend. In fact, Candy had tried to set me up with a friend of hers just a week before.

"You know," she prodded, as if I was to

43

guess exactly what vague idea she had rolling lazily around in that head of hers, "The guy who was watching you? With the baseball cap?"

The realization hit me like a train. My hands flew to my mouth. "Oh my god!" I shrieked. I'd purged him from my mind, written him off as a menstruation-inspired fantasy. But immediately every inch of my body began to tingle just imagining those hooded eyes exploring me. I wanted to see him. I had to see him.

"Where is he?" I begged hastily.

Candy shrugged and bit her lip. "Ummmmm…"

I blew right past her and bee lined it for the floor. He was not sneaking off again. I breezed through the entryway, a woman on a mission.

But Randy grabbed my arm. "Hey, I have a special job for you."

I barely looked at him, "Not right now, Randy, I have something I have to take care of."

He pulled my arm hard, slamming me against the door. "Not right now, you don't." The cheap scotch on his breath invaded my nostrils. "I have an important customer and he wants a private dance. From you. He is paying good money to see you, so you're doing this. Follow me."

Ah, fuck. The Pot. He must've snuck in on my break.

I felt my heart sink to my knees. The only thing worse than losing the opportunity to bore my eyes into my obsessive admirer was replacing that blissful anticipation with the morbidity of a private dance for a man I despised.

God, I hate my job sometimes.

Dejected, I followed Randy to one of the private rooms behind the bar and nodded to the bouncer who would be my only advocate for the next ten minutes. Randy remained by my side as I took my spot by the pole. Did he think I needed babysitting or something?

44

"This particular patron has a special request," he stated dispassionately. He held up his hands, atop which rested a long black bandana.

This guy had a thing for cowgirls? I can be so dense sometimes.

"He's a very private man. You will be well compensated." With that, he turned me around and proceeded to tie the bandana over my eyes.

What. The. Actual. Fuck. "Randy…you've got to be kidding me. This is a joke, right? You can't be serious. How am I going to see what I'm doing? What if he tries something?" I started to panic. I did not trust this man, and I wasn't just talking about the Pot.

"Fred is looking after you. You'll be fine. It's worth a nice pile of cash to you and a whole lot more to me."

I knew Randy had always valued money above all else but it was never a major motivator for me outside of the standard pay-the-bills crap. Still, if I was going to get through this, I knew I'd need an incentive. I took a deep breath and began visualizing what I'd buy with my blindfold money. A MacBook? Vacation? Add it to my savings?

I let these thoughts distract me as Randy's steps faded away. I was envisioning the upgrades I'd get on my new computer when a whispered conversation took place by the door and a new set of shoes entered the room. The footsteps sounded lighter than I expected, but of course, I'd never done this blindfolded before. I wrapped my hands around the bar, pulling my body into my normal introductory pose.

I stood statuesque until I heard the footsteps stop and the shuffling sounds of a body settle into the chair across from me. I started to move.

Huh. Much to my surprise, dancing was much easier blindfolded.

My signature daydream of Tom Hardy

45

sweating and glowering in the chair in front of me took over and I swayed into some sensual moves, enjoying the anonymity of my audience more than I expected. Tom was soon replaced with visions of my ball-capped admirer digging his eyes into me intimately. A picture of my true patron – the Pot – flicked briefly back into my mind.

My brain can be such a jerk sometimes.

I faltered at the image of the massive and dissonant man and scolded myself as I tripped on my heels. The sound of the Pot's shoes rang in my ears as they rapidly moved closer, no doubt to help me.

No! Don't touch me!

I cringed, resistant, but the hands that took hold of my arms to lift me back to my feet were not the chubby, sweaty, greedy hands I had expected. They were strong and calloused, but gentle.

It wasn't the Pot.

Fred rushed to my side in a flash, the sound of his heavy breathing all too familiar. "Do you need me to get rid of him?"

"It's ok, Fred," I said. "This is ok with me."

I listened. No footsteps, just a gruff grunt. He was hesitating.

"Really, Fred, I'm okay."

He sighed. "You let me know the moment you need me".

I listened as he retreated to his post by the door.

The patron's hand was still on my arm as I regained focus. In an uncharacteristic act of boldness, I placed my hand on his arm.

I had to know.

I moved my hand up his arm, running my fingers over the muscles and veins protruding from his rough skin. This definitely was not the person I had feared it was. I hesitated as my hand reached his shoulders – this was not included on the "good girl" list of our code of ethics (I know, the irony is

46

part of the fun); Randy might yell at me again. But then again, he clearly valued this man in front of me who hadn't moved from his spot since I began my limb groping so maybe I could get away with it.

My breath caught as he grasped my right hand softly, lifted it towards his face, and whispered, "Is this okay?"

I nodded. A massive lump of nerves had suddenly inexplicably incapacitated my throat. I stood stock still as he brought my hand to his face and placed it lightly on his stubble. I stroked his chin with my thumb.

He wanted me to know he was not the Pot. How did he know I needed that information? I caressed his face, feeling his eyes, nose and cheeks. I didn't dare touch his lips, desperately though I wanted to. He reached for my hand again, moving it upward to where, finally, I found my fingers resting upon the solid bill of a baseball cap. My heart stopped.

47

Chapter 6

A few swallows. A deep breath. Keep it together, Ellie.

I could almost feel his smile.

"Everything okay, Nevaeh?"

Good God, I loved the way his voice purred my name. He was teasing me, I knew it, but my elation at finding him here in place of my nemesis was far too pleasing for me to care. I smiled and nodded again. He then stroked my neck and chin with his hand, my skin glowing at his touch. He reached for my face – I dodged his hand, backing behind the pole.

"Sorry," he whispered.

"Randy told you my rules," I said, dejected.

My demeanor quickly tanked. This whole situation was ridiculous; why did he get to see me when I couldn't see him? It was bullshit. I was a fucking professional.

I pursed my lips and pushed him backward so I could get back to my job. I grabbed the pole ferociously and wrapped my leg around it, hoping

48

he could see the scowl on my face. He didn't say anything, which only served to piss me off even more.

"So this is how you like your strippers, is it? Makes you feel powerful? Some kind of fetish?" I swooped and spun low on the bar, my anger fueling my movements.

He chuckled. "If I had a power fetish, that blindfold wouldn't be around your eyes."

I stood up with a gasp. "Where would it be exactly? Up your ass?"

He paused. "Is that how you like it, Tiger Lilly?" He thought this was joke.

I could feel the smoke shooting out from my ears. "You know, most guys skip the hog-tying and just try watching strippers dance with their fucking mouths shut."

"Maybe I like it this way." He placed his hand over mine on the bar and leaned in. "How do you like it, beautiful?"

I recoiled, pulling my hand out from under his. "Talk to me face-to-face and I'll answer that question for you." I placed my hand on my hip.

He chuckled. "So is this some kind of special package? I get to listen to you bitch and whine while I watch you dance? Because, I have to admit, I kinda like it."

I could have killed him. I couldn't see a damned thing but I knew he was smiling. "You like it, do you? Another kinky fetish of yours?"

"It's growing on me."

"You can get much cheaper and far more interesting conversation over at Helena's."

Helena's was a nearby club well known in Vegas for its add-on escort services. It was not uncommon for the strippers to simply leave with their patrons throughout the night – they had a rolling on-call replacement system for their dancers.

"Nah, I kinda like you. In fact, maybe I'll

49

extend this little rendezvous. I want three songs."

I scoffed. "No. In fact, just get another girl. I'm sure you can find someone else in here who thinks being blindfolded is a turn-on."

I turned to leave, but he grabbed my hand, interlacing his fingers, and pulled me back, so close that I could feel his lips against my ear as he whispered, "I asked for you for a reason; I don't want anyone else."

Oh, I wanted so badly to keep being mad at him. I wanted to hate him, loathe him even. But something about his voice and his lips on my ear…it melted me into an Ellie-shaped pile of goo.

"Why?" I breathed, immediately kicking myself for allowing my vulnerability to peek through.

He didn't answer, but held me close for a moment longer before releasing me. "Please, keep dancing."

I was a bit uncertain at first. I wasn't used to being disarmed so easily. My brain thought to rebel, but my body wanted to make him hot and heavy, to punish him with desire. As I reluctantly worked my way back into my routine, my instincts took over. I worked the pole slowly, rolling my pelvis up and down, ruffling my hair, and enjoying every minute of my exhibitionism. I peeled my clothes off one by one, all the way down to my top and g-string, keeping a torturously slow rhythm to draw out his excitement. I wanted so badly for him to be rock hard. I wanted him want me so bad that it would kill him to know he couldn't have me.

My moment came. I heard him step towards me, this time more cautiously. He didn't move any closer; somehow I knew he was awaiting my permission. I reached my hand back, and groped for him. When I found his hand, I placed it lightly on my hip, just overtop my g-string, and repeated the action with his other hand. I could hear his breath take, and I felt his fingers twitch nervously.

50

His heat soothed me to the core; I wanted to evaporate right into him. I began to move.

He moved with me – quite impressively actually. Some men have a really hard time with smooth, sexy movements – they rock their hips like they're doing an amateur robot dance – but his movements were fluid and oh, so sensual. I drank in the feel of his fingers on my skin. My observation from the stage the other night had been correct: they were strong and slender, though minimally insecure. I couldn't blame him for that. Men had been kicked out indefinitely for this before. But I had worked with Fred for a while and he knew I'd signal if things got out of hand.

My admirer pulled me even closer against his body. I ground into him, low and deep. He followed me down, his breath on my neck as we rose back up. He nuzzled my hair with his nose and inhaled deeply as if to memorize the scent. We continued to rub against each other, each movement more intimate than the last. His hands crawled slowly up my hips to my bare belly as we danced. His pinkie finger slipped discreetly into my belly button, giving me a little tickle. I giggled.

"I've been wanting to touch that belly button," he whispered.

How adorable: a belly button enthusiast.

"It's unfortunate I can't return the favor," I mewed, too caught up in the moment to infuse the appropriate level of cynicism. I bent at the waist and reached for the floor, my butt still grinding at his pelvis.

God, it was so much fun.

He laughed. "I wouldn't have taken you for a twerker."

He rested his index finger where my spine met the base of my neck and trailed it softly down each vertebra until he reached the edge of my g-string. He traced the lace back around to my belly, pulled me in even tighter than before, and then we

51

rolled with each other again. His hands rubbed me more deeply this time, tracing a pattern from my hips to my shoulder blades and back again. I wanted him to reach for more but I knew he wouldn't. I don't know how I knew – call it instinct – but I was right. He didn't stray into any clothed territory.

I knew our time was drawing short. My desire to leave him wanting and unsatisfied was waning, thwarted by the fact that I wanted him too. Badly. I turned to face him and ran my hands up his arms and across his chest. Even through his t-shirt, I could tell he was in good shape. He tucked a stray hair behind my ear and for a moment I thought he might kiss me. The thought excited and terrified me in equal measure. I placed my hand softly in his. As I ran my fingers over his skin, I came across an unexpected stump at the end of his middle finger. My forehead crinkled in confusion as I rubbed my fingers over the end to confirm that the tip – from the third knuckle up – was indeed missing.

"Steel mill accident," he whispered.

So he's an industrial worker.

He tipped my chin back and attempted one more time to cup my face in his hand.

I blanched and shoved him backwards. "You think that just because I danced with you, you get to break my fucking rules? I told you where I stand; either get with the program or get the hell out."

"Jesus, calm down, it was an accident. Most women like it when I touch their–

"I don't care what it was. Just…keep your hands to yourself." I turned away with a huff.

I didn't hear anything but an exasperated sigh escape his mouth. Something slapped the ground and then, to my great disappointment, his footsteps faded towards the door.

Shit. What was I doing? What if I never saw

52

him again? Why do I always have to freak out over my stupid rules?

I thought about chasing after him and trying to fix the situation. I wanted him to come back; I wanted to give him the three dances he'd requested. But my pride wouldn't let me. Instead, I listened to the door slam behind him, then untied and chucked the bandanna as menacingly as I could. It landed on the cement next to a small pile of cash bound with a rubber band. I picked it up and found a stack of bills; one hundred dollar bills. Ten of them to be exact.

I was flabbergasted. Who was that? Was he…? Did he…? What the fuck just happened? Would he come back?

I sank to the floor. I felt defeated, maybe even a little silly. Of course he wouldn't come back. Not for me, anyways. I was a stripper. He paid me for my services. End of story. If he ever even desired to come back after that little episode, he'd have his pick; there were plenty of other girls far more appealing than me.

My audience vacated, I headed towards the door to face the rest of the evening. As I walked out, I came face-to-face with Randy.

Fuck, he's probably pissed that I ran another one off.

But to my surprise, he smiled. "Great work, Nevaeh!" he congratulated. "I've got some cash for you before you leave. You'll want to take it straight to the ATM, if you know what I mean."

I looked at the bills cradled in my palm. There was more? I feigned a smile and tried to remind myself that I did it for the money in the first place. Silver lining.

"Look, you've done great tonight, why don't you handle the bar for the rest of the evening? The tips are decent tonight and you won't have to dance for your buddy over there."

I glanced over to see the Pot. So he *was*

53

there. He flashed me a hideous smile and I raced to the bar with intense relief. Silver lining indeed!

Candy accosted me halfway there. "Nevaeh, how was it? Tell me all about it! Did you see him? What does he look like? Did he get your number? Are you gonna go out with him?" This girl was so naive sometimes.

I groaned, "Let me get to the bar and then I'll fill you in." I threw on an apron, excused Rain back to the dance floor, and turned back to an eager and anxious Candy. "It's no big deal," I muttered. "I had to wear a blindfold so I didn't see him. And he left early. So I don't really know what that whole thing was all about."

I didn't want her to know the intimate details of our encounter. It would only prompt more questions and plus... I kind of liked it being my own little secret.

Candy's face fell as if I'd just revealed that Santa Claus isn't real. "Blindfolded? Are they allowed to do that? Why did he leave? What are you going to do? What if he doesn't come back?"

I massaged my temples; I didn't have the patience for this. "Candy, I'm fine. Just get back to work, okay? We've got customers waiting." I turned my back on her to fill cocktails and she slinked back to the floor.

At closing, I was one of the last to leave. I was okay with that. I wanted to keep my mind busy and going home early would have thwarted that plan. Mia was the only other dancer left, off flirting with Randy somewhere. I really didn't understand what she saw in him. I guess he had some redeemable moments. He did seem legitimately grateful this evening. Maybe he was under more stress than I realized.

I finished sweeping, changed back into my jeans and t-shirt, and opened the back door, ready to head out to the far lot across the street. The evening would have been peaceful anywhere else,

54

but the poorly lit streetlights that cast nebulous shadows across the alleyway behind the club always quashed any feelings of security that might give way to enjoyment of the deep night sky. I took a step into the alley. From the corner of my eye, I saw movement. My eyes raced to catch sight of a shadow that I thought had flickered around the side of the building.

Nothing.

I reached my hand in my bag where my ridiculously stupid little girly gun sat. My hand bypassed it, however, and reached for my pocketknife. We all had at least one weapon for our own protection. Randy insisted on it and in that moment I felt grateful; perhaps he did care just a little bit. But I also felt a tinge of regret: I'd much rather have had access to the cold steel of a Glock G43.

I took a couple more cautious steps toward the corner, angling my direction outward to avoid any surprises. A moment's pause to listen for movement...still nothing. There was a teeny tiny part of me that hoped it was my ball-capped stalker, but the more practical side of my brain knew the more likely scenario was that a desperate and insecure admirer with a lack of patience for the word "no" was waiting despondently for me. I took another step forward just to be sure...

I think I'm just going to pause there. That's a good place, right?

Oh, get over yourself! I've been sitting with my ass on this hard bench for over an hour now, I'm hungry, over-coffee'ed, pissed off, and frankly ready to graduate from caffeinated hot beverages to more adult fare. Trust me, this story will get waaaaaaaaaaay more interesting once I have a fucking margarita in my hand.

I stand up, just a little bit wobbly from all the caffeine, and waddle my way over to the terminal's nearest bar. I order a margarita on the

55

rocks from the cute bartender and I'm half-tempted to ask him if I can have him on the side. But I resist. I'm not quite prepared to tell a sex story in the present tense.

Don't pretend you wouldn't like it, ladies.

I take a sip. And another. Maybe a couple more. Aaaaaaaaah. Ok, girls, *now* we can really get into the good stuff!

There was no one in the alley, by the way. At least not that I could see.

Disappointed, are you? I'm very flattered that you're so anxious to see me flogged and dragged away by a complete stranger, really I am, but you'll forgive me for not throwing my life at the feet of a crazed and horny psycho for your own personal entertainment. Wait, I'm a stripper... Okay, you win this time.

Anyways, Mia and Randy came stumbling out the club door next, laughing raucously.

As usual, Randy started yelling at me. "Ellie, what the fuck are you doing out here by yourself?". He only calls me "Ellie" when he's *really* pissed. Sort of the pimp's version of the parental full name scolding, if you will. "You know the rules: you always leave in pairs. Do you have any idea how dangerous it could be out here this time of night?"

I looked at Mia, hoping for some defense but she just shrugged. "He's got a point" she seemed to say.

"Since you clearly have no fucking concern for your own safety, from now on you will check in with me before you leave." Despite his anger, I sensed a tone of authentic concern in his voice.

I'd never noticed this before. Was it new?

He shifted uncomfortably. "I'm liable for each one of you, okay? If any of you get hurt on my watch, it's my ass on the line."

It was kind of cute watching him attempting to recover from his brief moment of

56

vulnerability. I suppressed a giggle and winked at Mia.

"Come on," Randy mumbled, "we'll walk you to your car."

I headed home while Mia and Randy walked from my car to the bus stop, hand-in-hand. They really were quite good for each other, really. It would take a certain kind of person to see past the mask Randy put on – a facade I was still trying to understand – and no one more up to the task than the indomitable Mia.

I threw my hair back in a ponytail and navigated to the main thoroughfare for the drive to my warm, inviting, and most importantly deranged-customerless neighborhood.

Chapter 7

She pinched her cheeks as she stared into the shattered glass mirror. They glowed a perfect shade of pink, enhanced by the chilly night air. She adjusted her position to release her tights from the pull of the rough cement, smoothing the cloth of her leather skirt with her fingers as she kneeled. It was perhaps the last night she would have to be so adorned. Goosebumps scattered across her chest as the wind picked up and she turned back to the mirror, propping it up on an old shoebox. The cracks in the mirrors lined up perfectly with the features of her face – one splitting the space between her eyes, another cutting her lips exactly in half, and yet another trailing jaggedly up the side of her face. In the middle, atop her nose, was the source of the cracks where she had smashed the mirror with an old brick.

She turned her face sideways, examining the smooth perfection that earned her living. She regarded more closely the shards hanging loosely from the frame. Which one to choose? Which one was most ideally shaped for her mournful celebration? She picked at the crack on the left side of the mirror and pulled out a triangular piece that slit her finger. She held it up to her eyes, the green sparkling nicely in the scratched reflection. Her arm rose above her, her breath caught in her throat, and she stabbed…

After an afternoon of writing, I stood nervously on the porch, meticulously dressed to perfection in a cute but modest sundress, flats, and a headband. I clutched my bowl of potato salad and scraped my fingernails on the hard plastic to distract my mind from my nerves. Footsteps approached the door. I took a deep breath. "Just hang in there, relax, and don't cuss."

The door flew open. "Auntie Ellie!" A small blonde girl with braces and a really cute dress (seriously, where did she get it, I want one*)* threw her arms around me. I laughed and returned her hug as best I could while balancing my dinner contribution.

"Ellie, hi!" Another smiling face appeared behind the girl.

"Hi Mom," I said, barely masking my anxiety.

I grabbed my niece's small hand and stepped inside to hug my mother. I caught a glimpse of my dad in the backyard, taking advantage of another opportunity to use his new grill. A little toddler boy wandered around the backyard near my sister-in-law, wobbling like a drunken sailor. My brother was likely not far away. My mom invited me in, wiped her hands on her apron, and requested my help with the salad.

God, my family is so fucking traditional.

I walked through the finely decorated and spotless living area into the kitchen. You'd hardly know there was any cooking going on. Every dish was perfectly spaced, the counters clean, and bowls of sides and toppings laid out on the clothed kitchen table with the precision of a game of Tetris. I poked my head out the back door and nodded

59

hello to my sister-in-law, Jenny. She was perched on the back porch steps, her legs modestly pasted together beneath her knee-length flowered dress, and her long light brown hair sitting in a perfect ornate little French twist. She gave me a genuine smile followed by frantic, searching eye movement towards the house.

No, Jenny, I did not set up a stripper pole in the living room for your kids to play on...yet...

"Tommy's over by the garden," she explained, knowing as well as I did that we'd both rather pass the time swimming in mud-encrusted elephant dung than spend more than two minutes together.

I tiptoed around the side of the house where I found Tommy examining the garden. Oh, I had him good! I snuck up behind him and threw myself on his back, nearly sending him barreling into the tomatoes.

"Ellie! It's about fucking time," he cried as he laughed and wrestled me to the ground. When he stood back up, he pulled his baseball cap off and shoved it in the back pocket of his faded jeans, now crusted with dirt. His sad excuse for a "nice button-up shirt" sported grass stains, but he hardly seemed to notice.

God, it was nice to have at least one person here I could be myself with.

"Watch your mouth, young man!" I scolded. "Or no potato salad for you!"

He laughed again. "In that case: fuck, fuck, the fucking fuckers."

I cringed at the thought of his wife overhearing him, but at the same time, I kind of hoped she did.

He dragged me to my feet and pulled me in for a big hug. "Goddamnit, how long has it been since you visited? Those guys at the club must really like you for some reason."

I gave him a sturdy punch in the shoulder.

60

"At least someone likes me," I teased. "Where's Dad? He was by the grill when I came in."

"He probably stepped into 'the lieu'," he smirked.

Oh dear. Mom and Dad had taken a trip to Paris for their anniversary and, ever since, Dad had taken to calling everything by its French name. His way of bringing home a souvenir, I suppose?

We headed back around the house to the grill. My dad stepped out the back door looking very pleased with his smoking pile of meat. I gave him a hug and let him give me a tour of the various types of juicy flesh we had awaiting us for dinner.

After the dinner bell rang, we all crowded around the old dining room table we'd used since childhood. I sat next to my niece, Kendra. Opposite me were Tommy and Jenny with Mom and Dad bringing up the ends of the table and my nephew, Scott, making a mighty beautiful mess on the tray of his high chair off to Jenny's left. In front of me lay the juiciest most succulent burger I'd ever seen.

"You truly are an artist, Dad." I complimented.

A proud grin overtook his face. "Allons-y" he said. Several pairs of eyes rolled.

I didn't get home cooked meals too often. I made good enough money that I could eat out most meals and I typically only kept snacks and sandwich fixings around the house. A nice juicy non-fast food burger was a welcome entrant to my vacant belly. I savored every bite as Tommy went on about his work at the engineering firm and dad drawled about the trip to Paris.

I didn't finish my burger. I couldn't. Not that I didn't want to, but I could only imagine the discomfort of trying to pull myself up and down a pole the following day with a huge burger digesting in the pits of my bowels... No. Just half.

The pitfalls of being a stripper.

"I'm looking forward to voting for

61

Anderson," my dad continued as my attention veered back to the dinner conversation. "We need someone like him in office to clean things up." Jenny and mom both nodded in agreement.

"He's such a nice looking man, too." My mom giggled.

"Oh come on, Mom, really? You're going to choose your political candidates based on looks?" I teased.

"Well, can you even imagine having to look at Boswell's face every day? We'd lose political interest on that fact alone!"

We all laughed and Jenny launched into a speech about her support of Anderson's social politics. Tommy nodded even though I knew he didn't agree – actually he didn't really care much for politics in general. Which was probably a good thing for the sake of their relationship.

"You can really tell an honest candidate by the way they carry themselves," Dad commented, his eyes on me. He knew I was his only opposition in the room. "Anderson speaks openly and carries himself with class. Boswell, on the other hand, gives me the distinct impression that he's hiding something."

I shrugged. "Maybe. But the real mark of a good candidate is the role of their spouse."

Jenny's ears perked up.

"Look at Boswell's wife," I continued. "She's involved in his campaign, giving speeches, writing books, and speaking intelligently on the subject of politics. She doesn't just stand there and daintily applaud her husband; she gets shit done."

My dad shifted uncomfortably in his chair.

I ignored him. "Look at Anderson's wife – actually, it's hard to look at her because she's never around." I laughed.

Silence ensued.

Oops. I cleared my throat. "She's completely uninvolved and uninterested in what happens in

62

her own town. And he's clearly never asked her to share her opinion on any prevailing issues. He shuts her away behind a locked door."

"Sometimes Moms have more important things to focus on," Jenny suggested, gesturing towards her kids.

I nodded. "Perhaps. But they don't have any kids. So where does that leave her?"

Another uncomfortable silence.

I decided to round off my end of the discussion. "Well, anyways, I don't think there exists an honest politician in the first place, so I'm not sure it even matters who gets elected."

"Speaking of dirty politicians…" Tommy piped in with a political joke he'd read on Facebook and the conversation moved on to other things, namely Tommy's recent promotion and Kendra's first days of second grade.

"Sounds like things are going very well for you, Tommy," Mom cajoled. She turned to me. "How are things going for you, Ellie? How is...um, well..." Her eyes darted around the room nervously, desperately seeking some subject she could ask me about that wouldn't make her look like a judgmental ass.

Too late.

Flustered, she finally blurted out, "How are things at the house?"

It was like this every time. My family members weren't ones to attack a subject head-on so it was difficult to try to discuss their discomfort with my career decisions in any productive terms.

"Things at work are fine, Mom," I finally said.

Her face glowed crimson. *For God's sake, it's just a job.*

I consciously perked up and sat forward. "In fact, I got to give the mayor a lap dance last month. Quite the squirmy guy for a married republican. Had no idea his interests were so

63

diverse."

Jenny choked on her burger.

Mom and Dad froze.

Tommy started laughing. "I knew it!" he cried. "That rat bastard. Not a word of truth comes out of his mouth."

Jenny kicked him under the table and he scowled, but tossed me a wink when Jenny wasn't looking. I picked up my plate and walked it to the sink, enjoying the heat from my parents' embarrassment that radiated into the back of my head.

Yeah, ok, I probably went a little far. But there's really only so much condescension and intolerance I can handle. This was my fucking life. Deal with it or disown me.

When I sat back down, Mom and Dad had started to recover, but Jenny glowered at me.

"Kendra," she commanded, eyeing her daughter sitting next to me, "Come sit over here by mommy."

"But I'm not done." Kendra whined.

"Now."

Kendra picked up her plate and moved around the table.

I scoffed. "Come on, Jenny, are you serious? Stripping isn't contagious, you know."

"You can't talk about stuff like that around kids," she seethed, her hands covering Kendra's ears. "I won't have her exposed to your...lifestyle."

"Jenny, I can only say this so many times before I lose hope that you will ever understand: my work and my life with my family are separate things. I will never reveal the gory details of my work with your kids around and I will never ask you to come for a friendly visit with me and my whores."

"Don't say that word!" she cried, increasing her grip on Kendra's ears until she cried out. She lowered her voice to a whisper. "If you only knew

64

how badly you need Jesus in your life..."

I made a big display of rolling my eyes. "Jesus fucking Christ…"

Jenny jumped to her feet. "Tommy, it's time to go. Ellie, I've had enough disrespect. Stay away from my kids, please, until you can learn to clean up that mouth."

My face flushed red with embarrassment and horror. "Excuse me? I'm their aunt! What on earth could I do to them that would be so bad?"

"I will pray for you," was her only response. She exchanged a knowing glance with Mom.

The dagger in my back twisted. "You know what? No," I announced, defiantly, "*I'll* leave. Clearly you're not the only one who's not comfortable having me here."

I glared at my parents as I collected my potato salad. They stared into their plates while I stormed out.

I got about halfway down the driveway when I heard Tommy behind me. "Ellie! For God's sake, wait!"

"I don't want to hear you defend her," I snapped. "How on earth did you end up married to that bitch anyways? She has no right! I've been nothing but wonderful to those kids." I choked on the last word as tears snuck their way out of my eyelids and onto my cheeks.

"Come on, Ellie, you know how she is," Tommy sighed. "She's just angry, she'll get over it. I'll talk to her later. Just please don't be mad. If you guys would just try for one fucking second to understand…"

"I am not the problem here, Tommy. Don't even go there right now. I love you, Tommy, and I love the kids, but..."

"I know..." he conceded.

"I can only handle so much berating and insults. I don't know what to do anymore..." I trailed off. I just wanted to leave; to go home and

65

curl up on my soft bed and pretend I had no family at all.

"I'll talk to her, okay? I promise. Just don't be mad at me."

"I could never be mad at you." I gave him a warm hug. I couldn't even remember the last time I'd been angry with Tommy. He'd been my best friend for most of my life. "Now get back in there and clean up my mess. You've always been good at that."

He heaved a relenting sigh and rolled his eyes. "Yeah, yeah, yeah…" He ran back inside.

I slumped dejectedly into my car.

Well, at least I had Tommy.

Chapter 8

It hadn't exactly been a good week. Sunday was the family my-daughter-is-a-slut disaster and Monday was booked solid with my recovery from said disaster, mostly consisting of a very long run, music videos on YouTube, and lots of writing. I tried to watch TV but the political propaganda was *not* something I had patience for.

As things wound down to a close at work that night, I was finally in good spirits. The clientele had been enjoyable and respectful, the tips were great, and I hadn't thought about my family or my frustratingly fascinating ball-capped friend since I had arrived. Mia, Randy, and I were left to close up for the night.

"Girls, I'm sorry but I have to ask you a favor," Randy sulked. "I've got to meet my ex-wife early tomorrow to pick up my daughter. It would be best if I looked mildly human when I do that so I need to catch some z's."

Mia looked disappointed but piped in. "Go ahead, Randy, we can finish up here. "

He nodded, grabbed his jacket, then stopped short. "Just please, *please* promise me you will both leave the club together?" he pleaded. "And Ellie, give Mia a ride home. It's late for her to be walking to the bus stop."

I nodded with a smile. It was nice to be called by my real name when he wasn't yelling at me. He gave Mia a grateful look and skipped out to the back room. Mia and I got the floor picked up, organized, and the tables wiped down. She then turned to me with the same hopeful look I'd just seen on Randy's face. I grimaced.

"Can you finish up, Ellie? Please? I'm exhausted."

"It's fine, go. I only have the bar left to wipe down anyways." Randy's request popped back into my head. "But be careful. Randy will be super pissed if anything happens to you."

"You do the same, Ellie." And then she was gone, too.

Ten minutes later, the sticky bar finally bleached and smooth again, I ran back to the dressing room, threw on my denim shorts, and grabbed my favorite red purse, ready for my own repose. I stopped back into the club to flick the lights out and jogged out the door into the warm night air. The temperature was always perfect at night in the month of May. The days were blisteringly hot, but the nights were blissful – not too hot, not too cold – a rarity for Las Vegas. It was cathartic.

I turned to lock the door, but something stirred behind me. *I thought Mia went home?*

Two large hands grasped my shoulders, spun me around, and slammed me up against the door. An unwelcome chubby face stared me down with hedonistic pleasure. "Well, hello Ms. Tits. I've missed you."

I buoyed up my strength and shoved and flailed to get the three hundred and fifty-pound

68

mass of sweaty skin off me but I was pinned tight. After all the working out I did to stay in shape for this job, and I couldn't even budge a man who clearly hadn't exercised a day in his life? Mother Nature is such a bitch.

"Get the fuck off me!" I screamed.

The Pot just laughed. "Ain't no one gonna hear you out here, missy. And anyone who does won't give a damn." He shoved himself harder against me, his face hovering centimeters from mine, his tongue tasting the tip of my nose.

"Didn't you get enough last time?" I cried in disgust. "What the hell do you want?"

He paused as I shut my eyes and squirmed as far away from his face as I could. He released a sigh that was sickeningly satisfied.

"I like it when you struggle," he breathed, his eyes rolling back in his head with pleasure. "It reminds me of old times…"

So that was it. The bastard liked torturing women. Well, this wasn't going to end well.

He slipped his hand beneath my g-string.

"Look," I suggested, trying to keep my cool, "let's just go inside. There's more room in there. I'll do whatever you want me to."

He laughed heartily, spittle shooting out from his fat lips and landing on the cringing skin of my face. "No, this is how I want you." He inhaled sensually. "Right here, on the dirty sidewalk, squirming and screaming...begging me..." He expired again with a shiver. "...covered in nothing but me and the filth of your livelihood. I never should have let you get away."

Like he could've kept me anywhere near him after that Mud Room experience.

I was going to pass out. The smell of his putrid sweat, the ambient light from the one bulb that hung loosely over the club door, the suffocation of his body cutting off my circulation...

Maybe this is a good thing. He likes a fight, and

69

I certainly can't fight if I pass out.

I waited for my knees to buckle.

Crack!

My eyes flew open as the deafening noise filled my ears. I knew that sound; it was unmistakable. I saw the Pot's eyes widen in shock. His hold on me eased and he convulsed as he dragged me beneath him to the ground. He was completely limp. If I'd had my sense of humor about me, I'd have enjoyed the irony but as it was, I was in a panic. The shear weight of his person held me prisoner against the concrete. I couldn't move him any more now than I could when he was muscling me up against the wall. I pushed on his chest, becoming more confused and disoriented by the second. My hand slipped and squished against something wet. Something red.

Oh.

Shit.

"Ellie! Oh my God, are you okay?"

I couldn't see much but I knew Mia's voice like the back of my hand. How did she always know when I was in trouble?

I grunted in response, my breath coming in small spurts.

"Oh my god, oh my god, oh my god..." she muttered as she yanked and pulled at the Pot.

Blood stained my clothes and I wasn't coherent enough to aid in my own rescue. "Just get him the fuck off me!" I cried, as tears started down my cheeks.

Mia tugged harder but she wasn't strong enough to handle such body mass on her own. I focused hard, mustering every ounce of strength I could find in any available crevice of my body. Mia counted to three and I heaved all my muscle against the Pot.

It was just enough. He rolled off me and I staggered, relieved but terrified, to my feet.

I backed up against the club door, my head

70

shaking and my pulse off the radar. "Is he...did you..? I–He–Mia, what the fuck?"

My hands held my face as I ached to understand what I had just experienced. The shock coursing through my body numbed me so badly I didn't even notice the blood that streaked through my hair as I rabidly tugged at it.

Mia was surprisingly calm. "Come on. We have to figure out a way to get rid of the body."

What? Get rid of the body? She thought we were criminals? "Mia," I stuttered. "Come on – he attacked me. Let's just call the police. Fuck..."

A small bubble of blood emanated from the gunshot wound in his back. I felt sick. I prepared to vomit.

Mia shot me a piercing look. "Don't you dare get sick, Ellie. You keep your shit together. Now. We can't leave any evidence."

I didn't move. I wasn't sure I remembered how.

"Ellie! Wake the hell up!" She was shaking me now. "I shot him, ok? He's dead. Get over it and focus on what we have to do next. Just like the time you had to dance for him. Just... pretend you're in a movie, remember?"

A movie. Yeah, a movie. Ok, I could do that.

I looked around nervously, desperate to avoid being a liability, but my mind was blank. I had no idea what to do.

"The trash can," Mia said. She pointed straight across from the club door where a huge green industrial trash bin sat. "Come on, we have to get him into it."

She was crazy; I knew it. This whole fucked up situation was crazy. We barely got the guy off me; how on God's green earth were we going to lift him into a trashcan?

I held my ground, shaking my head vigorously. "We can't..." I mumbled. I suddenly felt irritatingly cold. Like a frost had spread through

71

my limbs, weakening me and strangling me. My breath quickened.

Something changed on Mia's face in that moment, something I'd never seen before. Her jaw set, her back straightened, and her eyes became fierce. Her blurry profile walked back towards me and looked me in the eye, point blank, her voice steady and authoritative.

"Ellie. If you don't get your shit together now, we are going to end up in prison. Don't you remember Hannah? They said she asked for it. The law gives zero fucks about strippers. So you either bitch and whine your way home like a little baby girl while I clean up your mess, or you get your fucking feet on the ground, grow the fuck up, and get a vagina."

And then it happened. I looked closely at the Pot, stared deep into his eyes. The hate I felt for him coupled with the strain of Mia's words overcame me and my brain switched frequencies. My eyes cleared and my mind went blank, but in a different way this time. I lost track of all thought or fear. I could see every pore on Mia's face, every pebble on the asphalt, every scratch and dent in the trashcan. My nerves jumped to life as adrenaline began to pump through my veins once more. Nothing mattered except getting through this. Nothing mattered except surviving.

I reached into my purse and pulled out my pocketknife, released the blade, and secured my hand tightly around the hilt.

That's the last thing I remember.

72

Chapter 9

No, I'm not teasing you; I really, truly remembered nothing and I don't know why. It was pungently disturbing to come back to consciousness on my bed the next morning with no recollection of the events the night before.

I was groggy. My head hurt. I brushed a sore spot with my hand and winced.

Shit. It felt incredibly tender. I got up slowly, my back threatening to give out entirely as I hobbled to the bathroom. I looked in the mirror. My skin was completely covered in dried blood, my pajamas resting fresh and untainted overtop. It was a horrific image; a zombie-fied version of myself I never imagined I'd see. I immediately grabbed a towel and ran it under the sink. I had to get rid of the blood.

I cleaned off my face, arms, and chest. There didn't appear to be any visual cuts or bruises. I could only suppose it wasn't my own blood. Whose blood was it? I determined it must've been the Pot's blood, but…why so much? It was just a

73

gunshot wound.

I touched my head further towards the back – there it was. The tender spot. I parted my hair to find a swollen black, blue, and purple wound. It looked like the skin had been broken but not quite enough to merit stitches. A hard and craggy scab inhabited the middle of the bruise.

With a groan, I leaned my forehead against the mirror, shut my eyes, and concentrated on remembering how this had happened. I jumped as visions of the Pot and his seeping gunshot wound came back to mind.

I ran straight to the toilet.

As I cleaned myself up, my head started to clear a little bit. *Mia must be a pretty damned good shot.*

In a flash, I threw off my pajama top and felt around my waist, thighs, and pelvis. Nothing. Just my skin. Yep, she didn't even graze me.

I leaned on the bathroom counter. The Pot fell on me; I definitely remembered that. We managed to roll him off, then...what? What happened next? I willed my brain to remember. I could recall looking at the trash can across the alley...

"God damnit Ellie!" I pounded the counter in frustration, but it didn't help. Nothing helped. I threw my hand soap container across the bathroom and turned on the shower.

The warm water was like therapy, the soft dribbles tantalizing me with a gentle touch. A few trickles of blood washed out of my hair and down the drain. I was just starting to dip into a semi-meditative state when I realized something: my clothes. What had happened to my clothes? They must have been covered in blood. Surely they could be held as evidence or identify me as a witness. I wouldn't rat out Mia, but I didn't want to have to lie to the police either.

I hopped out of the shower, forgetting how

74

blissful my clenched muscles felt under the therapeutic water. I threw on my towel searched around the room. I remembered what I had worn the night before – my striped long sleeved top and my favorite denim shorts – but the clothes weren't there, clean or dirty. I searched my car as well, the neighbor boys surely enjoying my performance in nothing but a towel.

Nothing there, either. I didn't know where else to look. I had wandered back inside my house when I heard my cell phone ring upstairs. My heart lurched. Did I want to answer it? What if it was the police? What if it was Mia? Oh my God, was that Mia's blood all over me? *Please, God, no!*

I launched myself up the stairs to my room and found my cell phone by the bed, the word "Mia" flashing with the ringtone. I heaved a sigh of relief and picked it up. "Mia? Mia, are you okay?"

She responded immediately. "Yes, yes, of course. I'm fine, Ellie. I wanted to make sure you're okay. You were a little bit of a...mess…last night."

"I'm okay, I think." I said. "My head hurts but it's nothing a few over-the-counter drugs can't resolve."

Mia exhaled with relief. "Oh, good. I was worried about you. I thought the whole situation may have been, you know, a little too much for you. Especially considering…" she paused. "Ellie, you haven't said anything to anyone, right? You went straight home last night?"

"No. No, of course I haven't said anything," I answered, confused. *Especially considering what?* "Mia, what happened? I can't remember anything."

"Exactly, Ellie. I knew I could count on you. Are you working tonight?" Mia blazed forward at warp speed.

"I…You…What? Is today Wednesday?" I fumbled.

Mia laughed. "Okay, Ellie, I get it, you don't remember anything. Save it for the police."

75

I started. "Will the police be calling? I thought you said you didn't say anything! Why are they calling? What am I going to s –"?

"Ellie, Ellie, calm down! I haven't talked to the police; I was just using a figure of speech. We took care of things. No one is going to be calling."

I allowed myself to relax.

"But you should probably see a doctor, that was quite a fall you took."

I touched the bruise on my head. It definitely hurt, but I didn't want to see a doctor if I didn't have to. However, going to work like this seemed like a bad idea. How would I explain it? "I think I'm going to call in sick, Mia."

"No!" she cried.

I jumped.

"Don't do that! Randy doesn't know and if you call in he'll start asking questions. You have to stick it out, Ellie, just one night. Wednesday is your night off, right?"

I nodded. "Yeah..."

"Ok, good. I'll see you tonight, ok?"

"Yeah, see ya."

I tossed the phone on the bed. When it landed on the pale yellow sheets now stained a deep red, my eyes widened. The sheets were also covered in, well, *someone*'s blood. When would this nightmare end?

I ripped the blankets from the bed and threw them in the washer with two cups of soap and a healthy dose of bleach. I ran back to my bare bed and collapsed. I felt so confused. What was Mia's deal? Why was she suddenly insisting I go to work when moments before she was adamant that I should see a doctor?

And, of course, the big question: *what the fuck happened last night?*

My head was starting to hurt again. I grabbed a fleece blanket from my bottom drawer, pulled it over me and snuggled into my mattress. If

76

I was going to manage to survive a night at work, I would need some rest.

*   *   *   *   *

With the help of a little make up, some over-the-counter drugs, and a strong dose of determination, I walked into the club that night looking relatively normal. My nerves were on edge and my head was racing, but I thought I could hold it together as long as the night followed its usual course.

I didn't think about how stupid that was. I didn't consider for a moment that things never go the way they're supposed to when you're fucked up.

I groan loudly as I gulp down my third margarita. Time to pause the story yet again; I'm having too much fun getting drunk. Can you tell?

"Hey, hot stuff. You got another one of these back there?" I tease the handsome airport bartender.

He smiles and turns around to start me another drink.

"You don't happen to be meeting anyone here, do you? Perhaps someone you met at a strip club?"

He glances at me, but continues to give me the silent treatment. Figures. I'm not that lucky. I rest my head in my hands. I've given up at this point; clearly he isn't coming. I don't even want to look at the time to see how long I've been here. It really isn't fair. It truly seemed like there was hope, that this wasn't just my imagination.

I chug my last margarita, pay my tab (good thing I still have the presence of mind to do that!) and wander back to my bench. I glance at the newspaper sitting next to me. I laugh. God, I haven't touched one of these in years! Good thing about being drunk in an airport? Anything is interesting. I pick it up and leaf through.

I have the bench to myself now and it occurs to me that the two of us have become close. It perhaps doesn't realize how little intent I had on making it such an elongated resting place, but it is reality nevertheless. An idea pops into my head. I toss the paper aside and reach into my purse. I pull out the tiny pocketknife hidden in one of my keychains and dig into the wood. It cuts easily, if not slowly, as if it is welcoming my artistry. I want to make my mark; claim it as mine. After all, it may have much more drama through which to perservere. The least I can do is pretty it up.

Across the entire bench I carve, taking full advantage of the empty canvas. When I complete my work, a smile spreads across my face: not bad. Especially for a drunk chick. Across the surface cascades a number of successive lines about five inches in length, curved with the grace of a fallen leaf. Each line is accented with a number of perpendicular curly-queued designs that repeat from base to summit like an ornate one-legged ladder. I like it. I stash my knife back in my purse and admire momentarily, tempted to celebrate with another drink.

Wait, were you waiting on something? Oh yeah, my story! Bahahahaha! I completely forgot; silly me. Hang on. Let me release this burp digging into my lungs....ahhhhhhh.

Ok, so I was a total fucking idiot going to work after some crazy encounter that I couldn't remember with a dead fat guy which left me with a huge nugget on my head and a ridiculously sore back.

Sound about right? Is that where we left off? Certainly sounds like me...

I actually did okay at work for the first part of that night. Mia managed to talk Randy into giving me bar duty; something about my emotional state after a pregnancy scare (very creative, Mia)

78

but that only lasted a few hours. Some of the girls had an early night and, once again, I was on the late shift. Not the closing shift, luckily. Just two more hours and I'd be able to hit the road and hide away in my house until my memory resurged.

I went back on the floor and serviced a few lap dances, taking my turn at the pole while Mia took up bar duty. I was taking care of a particularly enthusiastic young man who clearly was new to the scene when Randy pulled me aside.

"Your 'special friend' is here again for his dance."

I panicked. No, the Pot was dead, wasn't he? Yes, I was sure of it. There was no way he had survived that. I thought. But I couldn't really remember.

God damnit, what happened?

Seeing my consternation, Randy filled in the blanks. "I was under the impression you liked this guy... the blindfold guy?"

Holy fuck. I'd totally forgotten about him. "I need to close this deal first. This guy might bust a nut if I don't finish him off."

Randy nodded. "I'll get him set up in the room. Meet outside the door in five."

I went back to my patron, my nerves buzzing beneath my skin. I felt like I should have been happy that my ball-capped stranger was there, but I was having a hard time figuring out how I felt about anything; I just felt anxious. And afraid.

My customer looked unusually relieved at my return. I gave him a nice butt-crunching final performance to which he decided to attempt some uncharacteristic boldness. His hand reached for my breast.

"Oh no, baby," I mewed, shaking my finger at him. "You know my rules; that's not part of the game." I continued my finale.

He tried again, this time getting a finger

79

under my top.

I glared. "Honey, I know you're new at this, but that's not how this works. You want hands-on, you pay for the Mud Room Special."

He grinned. What was wrong with this motherfucker? He was looking at me like I was teasing him. Was there a fucking smile on my face?

Reluctantly, I bent over again, ready to get this over with. He reached out a third time, only this time he dove into my top and palmed my boob, groaning.

In a nanosecond my hand was on his lapel. I lurched him out of his seat and across to the pillar behind me. He was a small guy, unfortunately for him. I shoved him against the cement. I could see nothing but a deadly red.

"What the fuck are you playing at?" I seethed.

His eyes darted across the room, his body stiff and unmoving. *That's right, motherfucker. How does it feel?*

I pulled him back and shoved him against the wall again. "Do have any clue what I could do to your tiny little dickless ass?"

Adrenaline was coursing through my body, giving me a power I had no idea I retained. And then Randy was on me. He pulled me off the little pipsqueak who ran out of the club with his tail between his legs.

"I dare you. I *dare* you to fuck with me again!" I cried after him.

"Ellie, for God's sake! Calm down! What the hell is wrong with you?"

I was still watching the door, rage pouring through my veins like poison. I wanted to chase him and rip his prissy little head off. Randy shook me again. Reality suddenly hit and the rage started to dissipate. I looked at Randy who struggled to keep a hold on me.

"Take five, Ellie. Now." He shoved me

80

toward the dressing room.

I faltered across the floor and through the door in a daze.

The girls were staring in shock as I entered the room and fell limp onto the couch. Mia ran in behind me, her eyes wide with warning.

I was too angry to waste time explaining. Yep, I was angry. Not regretful, just angry. Angry that Randy stopped me from ripping that fucker's face off. The thought of beating the crap out of any man who broke the rules filled me with satisfaction. It made me feel...powerful. I kinda liked it.

What the hell *was* wrong with me?

The grimace molded into my face didn't leave when Randy entered the room to scold me.

"Save it, Randy," I scoffed. "I know the rules – only guys get to stand up for themselves around here."

His face flushed. "Ellie, you need to go home now. You are in no position to be working here tonight. Take a couple of days and pull yourself together."

I almost grabbed my jacket and walked out right then and there, never to return. I'd had enough of this shit. But then I remembered the ball cap; my stranger was in a private room waiting for me. I couldn't even imagine leaving him there. I still wanted to see him again.

"You know I can't go, Randy. There's a guy waiting for me."

His shoulders fell.

Idiot.

He shook his head. "No, I'll have one of the other girls do it. You're not yourself right now." He gestured dismissively at me, one hand massaging his forehead. "Jesus, you look like you're ready to hit the gladiator ring."

One of the new girls, Yvette, who apparently felt like it was good weather for digging

81

her own grave, suddenly jumped up eagerly and screeched, "I'll do it, Randy!"

A hush fell over the room as every person took a step back. I turned my head slowly, my glare fixated directly on Yvette's perfect, shiny, innocent – and soon to be seriously fucked up – face. My eyes narrowed. If I hadn't been so royally pissed off, I probably would have enjoyed the terrified look on her face; it was rather humorous. But instead, I stared her down. I wanted her to see the heat running through my veins.

"Are you fucking kidding me?" I whispered.

She said nothing. I swear to God you could have split an atom with the look I was giving her. I stood and took several steps towards her until she cowered in the corner, muttering an incomprehensible apology. At that moment, it occurred to me that every girl in the room was watching me in shock.

Ok, show's over, ladies.

I turned back to Randy. "We both know he won't be okay with that, Randy. And we both know he's worth…" My eyes flitted around at our audience of underpaid strippers. I finished the phrase through clenched teeth. "…a lot of money to you."

He continued to hesitate.

"Goddamnit, Randy, it's not every night we get to see this kind of money. I'm going in there. Try and stop me."

He blocked my exit. I watched him wrestle with my argument, my toe creating a rhythmic echo on the cement floor. I could tell dollar signs were flapping through his brain en masse. He finally stepped aside and gestured back towards the floor. "Ladies first."

I exhaled; I hadn't realized I'd been holding my breath. I walked back to the floor with Randy at my heels. I stopped outside the private room by the

82

bar and waited obediently for him to tie on the bandanna.

Before opening the door, he leaned in and whispered, "don't you dare fuck this up."

Chapter 10

Randy walked me into the dark room – well, it was dark to me anyways. For all I knew the room was flooded with the angelic light of heaven. He led me to the pole and introduced me. "Nevaeh, sir."

Good Lord, he's so formal sometimes.

He walked away.

I stepped in the direction I thought the pole was but tripped on the base, almost face-planting into the cement floor before the Stranger caught me. He helped me up and I pulled myself ferociously from his grip. This blindfold thing was getting old fast.

"Let me go, I can make do." I spat.

"I'm not sure you can. You might consider a career change – maybe something where your feet stay firmly planted on the floor?"

"I'm *not* the one who asked to go into this blind."

He sighed. "Trust me, it's better this way."

"Fine," I threw my hands in the air. "Why

84

don't we just take this all the way, then? Do you want to chain my wrists too? Maybe throw a dog collar around my throat?"

An exasperated chuckle echoed across the room. "As amazing as that sounds, I think I'll just stick with the standard Dance & Sass package."

I paused, suppressing a smile. "The sass comes extra these days. You have to pay more if you want me to use my brain."

"Eh...maybe you can just shut up and stick to the dancing tonight then."

My face flattened and I balled my fists. *Fucker.*

I couldn't think of a retort so, with a huff, I moved to my starting pose and prepped for my nerves to return. They didn't. Not at all. In fact, I felt rather stalwart up there. Confident and poised, I bowed into a hip lock drop, starting my performance with one of the more difficult moves. The music piping in through the speakers was especially sensual so I took advantage.

My dancing that night was probably not much different than any other night; I was probably no sexier than before, but there was an added flavor to my aura. A little something extra. My transitions were just a little more fluid, my facial expressions right on cue, my movements just noticeably more sure. I could almost feel the energy that surged out from my body as I swung myself this way and that. I didn't falter. And more importantly, I knew I wouldn't. Handling the pole, the routine, the eyes watching me...it all seemed so...

Easy.

A few minutes into my act, I heard him approach me as he had during our first rendezvous. I didn't stop, but pretended not to notice.

He waited a few beats, caught me mid-swing, and pulled my backside against him, close enough to feel his warm breath on my neck.

Warm breath.

Like violent, piercing lightening I was transported back to that moment, suffocating against the wall with the Pot breathing on me, choking me. I fell to my hands and knees in the alley, coughing and gasping for breath as the smell of melting human flesh invaded my nostrils. My body collapsed on the asphalt, convulsing and threatening to shut down entirely.

"Nevaeh!" the Stranger said. "What the–

That soft sexy voice of my ball-capped stranger pulled me from my nightmare momentarily. I was still in the private room wearing the blindfold, but on my hands and knees choking. The blindfold remained an unwelcome prison wall between me and the face I needed so badly to see in that moment. My beautiful stranger touched my arm. It felt nice, soft and warm. He gave me a small squeeze and I was propelled back to the alley, the Pot on top of me, crushing me. A piercing pain filled my head and I began to scream as the smell of burning skin molested my nose once again.

I heard Mia yelling. "Ellie come on! Now! We have to go!"

I clasped my hands around either side of my head, screaming again as smoke filled my lungs.

"Ellie! Ellie!"

I don't know how long it lasted, but the torment finally began to fade and I looked up to see Randy, Mia, and some other guy gazing down at me intensely, wiping my head with a rag and calling my name. I came to just long enough to mumble "I'm fine," and then I was off in la-la land again.

This time the nightmare was gone and I was left with just hallucinations. I felt myself being carried. I looked up to see Paul Patson smiling

86

down at me, guitar in hand, singing a tune I couldn't hear. Then my father was there with Smith Anderson, scolding me for dancing with an injured head and trying to talk politics all at the same time. Then I saw Tommy. Sweet Tommy. I smiled up at him and he responded with a concerned grin. A tear dropped from the crease in his eye.

"Don't cry, Tommy," I tried to say.

I reached up to touch him but he moved, and then the Pot was above me. He was staring down at me, eyes still and stale, opened wide like a tortured rabbit but devoid of any nuance, for evil or for good. I gazed up at him, the horror of his bloodless face gripping me tightly until his hair turned to flames and he slowly faded away. I gladly faded with him.

*   *   *   *   *

Ouch. I hurt. My head hurt. Everything hurt.

I wrenched my heavy eyes open, terrified that I was splayed out on the concrete behind the club.

A soft mattress cradled my tired body. White sheets. Tubes. A box of tissues. I tried to sit up to get a better analysis of my surroundings but my body commanded me to stay put. I let my eyes rest shut as I listened for sounds that might give me clues as to where I was and with whom I might be.

Footsteps. I eased my eyes open just enough to see my mom walk into the small plainly decorated room with a drink in hand.

"Ellie!" She rushed to my side, pulled my hand into hers, and stroked my hair. "Thank God you're awake."

The hospital. This had to be the hospital. It definitely wasn't my mom's house. She wouldn't be caught dead with white walls in her sanctuary.

"Cliff!" she yelled. My father wasn't far

87

behind. "She's awake! Call Tommy."

My dad approached me and squeezed my arm. "That's my strong girl."

I was surprised to see tears prick his eyes. My strength began to return and my body responded to my commands once again. "Hi Daddy," I said.

His face scrunched. I hadn't called him "Daddy" for years. Just as I thought I might see him cry for the first time in my life, he hurried out the door to call Tommy.

"Mom?" I said, somewhat astounded by the hoarseness in my voice, "I feel like I should eat some Jell-O."

Mom smiled jovially. "Jell-O. That's funny. Good to see my little girl's sense of humor is in tact. I think you'll be alright."

I smiled. "Not if you don't get me some Jell-O."

She laughed.

My lips curled downward. "Seriously, mom, I'm fucking starving."

She winced, patted my hand, and set off to find the cafeteria.

I settled back into the pillow. My body felt like a long, skinny slab of cement that had just been poured, lazily waiting for paralysis to kick in. It felt great. I couldn't remember the last time I'd appreciated the comfort of a soft (well, mostly soft) bed and a fluffy pillow. I cooed to myself as I sprawled across the bed, my left leg slung lazily over my right.

Of course, then my brain started thinking again. *Damnit.* I started to consider what had happened. I had been dancing...where? Where was I? Oh yeah, the private room. The man in the baseball cap was there...nmmmmmm. He was so yummy. I laughed to myself. What kind of drugs did they have me on?

He had approached me...and then

88

everything went blank. Again. God damnit. My frustration went quickly from zero to one hundred. Why the fuck couldn't I remember anything?

I punched my pillow repeatedly, releasing my anger, frustration, and anxiety at the stupid, ridiculous, ass-fuck-worthy brain I had. How was I going to deal with any of this if I couldn't even fucking remember it?

Have you noticed yet that I like the word 'fuck'? It's not just because of its meaning. It's just the most cringe-worthy word that comes to mind when I'm so pissed off that every other word seems completely and utterly useless.

Fuck, fuck, fucking fuckery!!

My hospital stay was fairly uneventful: a lot of people doting over me, chastising me, and me doing a whole lot of lying. Mia had drummed up an excuse for my head injury and the subsequent delayed concussion that lead to my collapse and accompanying hallucinations at the club. Apparently when we were cleaning up the other night after Randy left, I had slipped on the mopped floor and slammed my head on one of the tables. Again.

Yep. No murderous clientele. No three hundred and fifty pounds of human fat that trapped and suffocated me. No obscure smell of melting flesh I couldn't understand nor chastise from my mind. I considered simply adopting this new story altogether, just convince my subconscious that it was nothing more than a bad fall on a wet floor. It seemed as good a solution as any.

Tommy and Mia were the only visitors I really appreciated. Tommy came by not long after Mom and Dad. He was in good spirits. Must have gotten laid.

"You're an idiot. Who gets a concussion by slipping on a wet floor?".

Well, no one, actually. "You know I was

89

always a klutz growing up," I chided.

"Yeah... Which really makes me wonder how you manage to hold a job as a dancer."

I couldn't hold back my smile. It was nice to be called a "dancer" every now and then. You know, as opposed to the less-flattering adjectives I usually received.

"But I'm not about to visit you at work to find out why..."

I giggled. "Psycho bitch wouldn't go too nuts..."

He glared. "Don't call her that." He paused, then flashed a sheepish grin. "Only I'm allowed to call her psycho-bitch. And I save that for the sack."

"Agh!" I shoved him back. "I don't need to know about your weird kinky bedroom pet names!"

Later, Jenny came by with the kids for a few minutes, bringing no apology for our last interaction. She sat down next to me and explained to Kendra and Scott that bad things like this happen when we don't follow God. I rolled my eyes. *Really.* She then reached for my hand; I thought she might be offering condolences.

I was stupid. She grasped her kids' hands and they bowed in prayer. I played along. At first.

"God, please help Ellie to give up her sinful ways and join us at church. Teach her to make good decisions and come back from the Devil's path..."

I stole my hand back from her. I couldn't take it anymore. Not one more moment. My adrenaline kicked in once again and rage coursed through my skin. No more being belittled. No more insults. I looked Jenny straight in the eye, hatred boiling in my veins. "Jenny: I've had it. Take your kids and get the *fuck* out of my room."

She stared at me, her eyes the size of bibles.

Kendra look frightened. I didn't give a damn. None of this shit was worth it anymore. I

90

wanted them out of my hair and out of my life. They were poison.

Jenny hesitated. She reached for my hand once again, a look of pity in her eyes. "It's not me, Ellie. It's God speaking through me."

I gestured at the door. "*Now*."

She stood and hustled her kids out the door, no doubt happy to have the excuse to keep them far, far away from me.

Fine. She could have it.

It wasn't an hour later that Mom and Dad stepped in to try to mend the break. After dodging questions and scowling for half an hour, I told them they were only allowed in my room if they talked about anything except Jenny. They complied after the deadly look I gave them the second time they tried, yet again, to sneak in the subject.

"She's just upset. Her head isn't right," I heard Mom mumble on her way out. "We can come see her in a few days after she's settled in back at home. At least she won't be able to go back to that job..."

Ha! I was going straight back to that job. I watched with pleasure as they left. I didn't even care to consider what their reaction might be when I broke the news. Hell, I didn't have to break the news, did I? It was my life, after all.

And where the fuck was the Jell-O? *I want some Jell-O, damnit!*

They only held me at the hospital for twenty-four hours. Hell, they didn't really do anything, just lots of monitoring and tests. I could've held a cool rag to my own head in the comfort of my home, but it made Mom and Dad feel better that I was there. Which meant they left me alone. I was happy with that. I didn't really feel like listening to them shit all over my career anyways. But I was very much looking forward to getting back to some normalcy; some regularity. Pretty much anything that would help me move on

91

from everything.

Chapter 11

That hospital visit sucked. It sucked even more than this airport sucks. Why did you make me tell that part of the story? It brings back all sorts of painful memories…

Ah fuck. Memories. Okay, sit down, I think it's time I let you in on a little secret. Actually, to everyone who has ever met me, it's no secret. Even my family knows and I don't even really like them. Well, I should say they *know* about the secret, but they don't know the *reason* for it. Pretty much everyone knows about it except you.

So it's confession time. I just…I feel like we've become close, you and me, as you've learned more about me through this story. And you're still with me, even after everything I've done, so that means I can pretty much trust you, right?

See here's the thing about stories. I'm good at telling stories for one specific reason: there are no pictures. You can't see me; I can't see you. No societal assumptions can get in our way, and no preconceived notions can halt our progress. It's great. We become besties in no time.

And usually that means I don't have to reveal my secret at all – you can pretend I'm perfect in every way and we're all happy!

Except, well, I'm drunk right now. And vulnerable. And maybe a little bit guilty – okay, a lot guilty. I've brought you this far on our journey and I've held back something that's fairly vital; something that might change the way you see me. But look, you can't really be angry that I haven't told you, I mean I work pretty damn hard to forget about it. And I haven't *completely* kept it from your awareness – I have eluded to it during my story here and there. You probably didn't notice because for the most part I pretend it's not there and act like it doesn't matter. As far as I'm concerned, at least when I'm sober, it doesn't exist.

But when I'm drunk it does. When I'm drunk I can't deny it for some reason. When I'm drunk I feel like I have to deal with it; face it. I can't pretend anymore.

I hate that.

A tear trickles down my cheek. I squish it with my finger and smear it down the side of my face right over my secret. My secret that is as plain as day and yet I still play the part as if I'm that perfect girl with the perfect body and the perfect skin and a perfect past. You'd think I would have learned by now.

Here goes. Deep breath.

A long time ago I went through some…traumatic experiences. I honestly can't even choke out the details right now; it hurts too much. I can't even begin to remember without flying into a rage. The reality of it grinds deeply into the pit of my stomach and whenever I think about it I feel like Satan is drilling a jagged hole through my soul. But you should at least know…sigh. You should at least know the evidence that was left behind. I think you've earned that.

94

It's my face. My once-adorable, squeezable face. My left cheekbone is the perfect image of flawlessness I'm sure you've always imagined (bahaha! Ok, I can pretend, can't I?). But on the right–

"Oh my God!!"

I look up. A strange old woman is standing in front of me, staring. God damnit, this is what I'm talking about. This is why I pretend it's not there.

"Are you okay, dear?"

I realize I've been balling. The sorrow in my face is probably a terrifying sight indeed.

"Honey, what happened to you?" She sits down next to me. "Why do you have that ugly scar on your face? Who did this to you?"

She is really damn lucky she caught me drunk. What an audacious bitch. But as it stands, the comfort is so, so welcome. So instead, shoving my shame deeper within, I bury my face in her shoulder, and let the tears run freely.

"Talk to me, dear," she whispers.

I shake my head. I can't. I may never be able to. The ugliness of this blemish has haunted me for years on end.

See, we're not just talking about a little spot on my face, a scab, or one or two stitches. This scar – this *thing* – runs from the top of my right cheekbone all the way down to the dimple next to my lip. It's hideous – a bit faded over the years, but still large, jagged, and impossible to miss.

Only at the club do I get to avoid conversation about it. It's the only place where it's too dark to see it. It's the only place where my body matters more than my face. It's the only place where there are people more fucked up than me...

So I'm sorry. I'm sorry I've cached this from sight for so long. If you can't read my story a moment longer, I understand. So much had happened even before that fateful day when the Pot attacked me and threw my life into disarray.

95

I promise I haven't hidden anything else about myself. You've seen all of me now – from the worst and most depraved things I've done to my sick and tarnished image.

But this thing. This one thing. This part of my past that has haunted me for years and will forever remain in my disfigured shadow...

I can't tell you any more. I've already said enough. The ache is starting to return and I can't go there, can't do it right now. I kiss the kind woman who offers me comfort and turn away. She pats me on the back, then admits that she has to get to her gate. I'm relieved. We've already spent more time discussing this than I've ever cared to.

Back to the story.

*   *   *   *   *

I finally went back to work four days later. It took some arguing, but the massive pile of money I'd made Randy the week before was his final undoing. He could never turn down cash. It was kind of annoying, but it got me what I wanted.

Of course, he and Mia offered me no aid in identifying the ball-capped stranger I'd become infatuated with. I knew they'd seen him point blank, but supposedly they had no information to offer me.

"It was a guy, Ellie. That's all I know," said Randy.

Mia just shrugged. "He was cute."

I told her I had seen Paul Patson after I fainted.

She just laughed. "As if..."

I sighed and Randy pointed irritably to the floor. "Get back to work. That's what you begged me to do, wasn't it?"

Gladly.

96

I'd like to say the following two weeks passed without incident, but that wouldn't be completely honest. I mean, aside from the fact that the ball-capped bastard didn't show up even once, in my mind those two weeks were fairly inconsequential. However, I don't think Randy or the girls would agree.

See, I just didn't really care anymore. Most everyone outside of our clientele became an annoyance. Actually, that's not entirely true; I did toss a beer in the face of one of my clients. Then punched him. Then threatened him with my hands clenched around his thick throat.

What? He was being disrespectful.

Randy tried to fire me again. I laughed in his face. That wasn't going to happen; he needed me and he knew it.

My parents tried to call me. I didn't answer. I had nothing to say to them. I talked to Tommy briefly, but as soon as he tried to bring up psycho-bitch, I hung up. Try again in ten years, buddy.

I started getting weekly massages. All of my stress seemed to carry in my back and it hurt like a mo-fo. Sometimes it felt like the Pot was still lying on top of me. Crushing me. I woke up every morning to the smell of his melting flesh. I didn't eat breakfast most mornings; I couldn't. It took at least a few hours to forget the odor. And knowing it would just come right back the next morning...

It wasn't very comforting.

Ok, I need a break from my sob story for a few minutes. Are you starting to feel sick? Because I am. Gaaaaaawd, I am so over my poor, sad, sucky life!

I glance at the newspaper on the bench next to me, but I suddenly can't bring myself to read it. Pain, suffering, and depression: that's all that awaits me between those expired black and white pieces of compressed recycled papery. Like I need anymore of that.

97

The old lady whose shoulder I bawled on is sitting a few benches down, waiting for her plane. She's probably afraid of me now. And hell, she's probably depressed too. Probably just like me, waiting for her knight in shining armor who has been leading her on for eighty years and now she's stuck, a lonesome and pitiful piece of shit, sitting in a dingy airport, and wishing she'd died during her last heart attack at Thanksgiving.

I suppress a snicker. There's no good reason for that to be funny right now. But God help me, it is.

I walk over to her, determined to give her my condolences for the shit situation we're in. "Look," I drawl as I clumsily sit down next to her, my words slurring just enough to give away my lack of sobriety, "you were kind to me before, so allow me to return the favor: He's a dick, ok?"

She looks up at me with eyes so innocent and pure.

"You deserve better, goddamnit," I continue, "your life isn't over! Go live a little. That guy over at the bar there, he'd make a good fuck. Go on, hit him up!"

She looks like she needs to get laid; it's the least I can do to thank her for comforting me in a down moment.

She regards me quizzically, seeming to consider my words. "Are you one of those airport whores?"

Huh? I double over, unable to contain my laughter.

Airport whore.

It's funny because it feels so true.

And then my laughter turns to tears and I'm sobbing. I fall into her arms *again*; the welcoming arms of this old, crusty, sweet-as-wine stranger, mumbling on about my love life (or lack thereof).

I doubt my words make any sense, but she strokes my hair and coos, "There, there. You won't be a whore forever."

"I don't want to be a whore forever!" I cry, my sobs turning to gulps and gasps. "He was going to save me! To take me away from all this!" I blow my nose on her knit sweater.

"I knitted that with my bare hands..." she mutters, but I pay no heed to her words.

I sit up and look her in the eye, grasping the edges of her face with both hands. "You are the real thing, Chloe."

"My name's not–

"No!" I scold, squeezing her face tighter, "You are whatever you want to be. Don't you dare give up." I look deep into her eyes, and then plant a long and sensual kiss on her wrinkly, decrepit lips. "You are worth a million dollars, Chloe. Even if he never shows up."

The shock in her eyes hits me like a semi truck and I realize she is not happy with my display of affection. I see security edging their way towards me from the corner of my eye and, with the last garnish of sense left in my inebriated psyche, I fucking run.

Luckily, security guards are apparently not as fast as drunk people.

I steal the paper from my special bench – good-bye bench. We had some lovely times together. We really did. I will miss you dearly. Don't forget about me when the next set of hot stripper cheeks lays stake to your hard but nurturing surface. I book it down the escalator and sneak in between the doors of the concourse tram just seconds before they close.

Like a boss.

I wave at the security guards staring at me through the glass. "Suckaaaaaaaas!"

The train lurches and I fall ungracefully into several fellow passengers.

"I'm not drunk," I assure. "I just... I got dumped. Ya know?"

99

I get a few sympathetic looks. Ah hell, they all love me. I can tell. I'm adorable.

I mosey off at the next stop and decide to play it cool for a little while by leaning inconspicuously against the bathroom sign. No one sees me here. It's like I'm part of the wall.

Shit! My bench! It's unmanned. What was I thinking? What if he actually shows up? I suddenly can't understand why I left. Sure, the night isn't looking like it will end well, but I can't take that chance. I cautiously make my way back to the tram and take the long way back to my concourse by returning to the terminal and then waiting in the agonizingly long security line again. When I arrive back, out of breath, I'm almost in a panic – but there's still no one there waiting for me. Did I miss him? I stare at the bench, dejected.

But what can I do? I already know I won't give up on this until the fat lady literally sings. No point fighting it. So I slam my ass cheeks back on the bench.

I look at you.

I'm sorry, were you hoping I'd continue the story? God, you are so fucking demanding. Can't you see I'm having an existential crisis? I have a headache, no less.

I stop in the convenience store for some drugs.

Really? You're still there?

I huff. Okay, but as I've mentioned before, the story doesn't get any better. And you're going to hate me.

Really?

You are incorrigible...

100

Chapter 12

It was time. The bodies had begun to overpower her will to kill and the past was catching up with furious ardor. She pulled the small wooden box from the depths of her bureau and opened it with ceremonial reverence. Each thick ring shone with heavenly splendor, animating her eyes and increasing the rate of her pulsating heart. She ran her fingers over each one – the silver ones, the gold ones, the titanium ones. Each had its own special and sentimental meaning. She could almost feel the stroke of their cold stiff fingers as she caressed her prizes. This was the one thing she couldn't take with her; the one thing that brought second thoughts and feelings of regret. She set the box down. Such a prize couldn't be wasted. No. At least not until the work was complete. She knew she'd never give herself in until every single craggy, blood-stained slot in that velvet-lined treasure chest was occupied.

Three weeks. Three weeks it had been since the awful event that I couldn't remember but also couldn't wipe from my mind. It was making me crazy. If I could remember it, I could resolve it all. Make sense of it. Move on. But fate wasn't having it.

So I was back at the club yet again, hoping I could keep my shit together. The girls avoided me. I could see the looks in their eyes – some of them afraid, some of them concerned, some even pissed off. I couldn't exactly blame them. Sweet, agreeable little Ellie was gone. Say hello to New Ellie who defends her territory, mouths off to girls who take her customers, and makes damn sure she makes the most money every night. For once I was in control. As much as I despised the shitty circumstances that brought me to that point, it was pretty fucking nice to be able to draw the attention of an entire room of strippers without waving so much as a one dollar bill.

Apparently my new attitude did something for the clientele too because I had become pretty hot stuff. I never imagined I'd ever scratch the surface of Mia's popularity, but I'd been moved to the top spot in the evening's introductions and spent more time on lap dances than ever before. I was number one. The best. Just like I'd planned.

It felt fucking amazing.

Mia was supportive, although she held some reservation about my behavior. Probably afraid I'd steal one of her regulars – ha! Like she could stop me. But more likely, she was still afraid I would squeal about our inconvenient murderous activities not long ago. God, did she have no faith in me at all?

Anyways, I was stalking a very nice looking older man with a lot of cash to disperse, flirting my little brains out, when I saw Randy staring at me across the room. He gestured to the bar and, with annoyance, I ambled over to join him.

"For God's sake, Randy, didn't you see his wallet? Leave me alone, I've got more fish to catch!"

He was unmoved. "I know you think you're

102

the shit now, but our very wealthy friend is back and I still need you to do your job with him."

"Wait, the blindfold guy?" My heart quickened. *God, give it a rest, Ellie, who cares? He disappeared for almost a month. He's just a fucker here to get his jollies; he has no interest in you.*

Randy nodded. "Think you can afford to spare Mr. Rogers over there for another thou?"

I stopped. I considered. Did I really want to see this guy again? I mean, he'd been messing with me for weeks and, whether or not it was all in my head, I knew that if I walked in that room I'd be hoping for more. More what? I didn't know. Just more. And I didn't think he had any interest in that. Not after the way he ditched me in my moment of need and then disappeared without a trace. But I had to admit: I missed him. I missed arguing with him and feeling his hands crawl all over me. Could I really blame him for running off? He was just a customer for fuck's sake. Everything else was just fairy dust I'd built up in my own head.

That's it; that was my problem. I made this out to be more than it was. It was time to face reality: I was a stripper entertaining a patron. No more. So I decided. I decided right then and there that I was going back. I was going to face him blind and vulnerable once again, but this time...this time I was going to prove it to myself. Prove to myself that I could let go of silly schoolgirl fantasies and have a raw, electric, sexy encounter with this stranger and ask for nothing more. I was going to beat him at his own Goddamn game.

"I take it you're going to take the thou?" Randy said impatiently.

I barely heard him. I was already on my way to the chilling and impassive private room behind the bar, prepared to greet my heartless nemesis with an equally glacial demeanor. I was going to fuck the hell out of that pole and I was going to enjoy every last sensation of the

103

experience, right down to the sexiness of the lashes on his straining wanton eyelids.

Randy had to run to keep up with me. He barely stopped me before I barged into the room to remind me of our distinguished guest's special request. My lips pursed as the bandana was tied around my head. Randy walked me in but I hardly needed his help. I knew exactly where I was and exactly where I planned to end up.

My confident swagger gave nothing away as to my earlier consternation. Even Randy seemed a bit off-keel at my behavior, stumbling over his words as he introduced me. If he could've seen my eyes, he would have surely recognized the "get the fuck out of here already" look as he lingered awkwardly following his shitty intro. As it were, the crease in my forehead and my tightly clenched lips seemed to be indication enough for him and he finally vacated the premises. I would have sent Fred along with him but I knew even new bitchy Ellie couldn't make that happen. Randy truly took no chances when it came it liability. Ahem, I mean safety.

I took my time getting started, teasing the pole with my fingers and staring dauntlessly in the assumed direction of my willing audience. I whipped my hair around, rolling my hips to the music before pulling myself flat and hard against the pole and sliding slowly down to the floor. This shit was going to make him blow.

I wasn't far into my titillating routine when I heard his footsteps approach me. Ha. No fainting halfwit here this time. *That dick had better be hard or I'm doubling my fee.*

Much to my surprise, he didn't touch me. He didn't say anything, at least not at first. He just stood there. He was within a foot of my sexiest most ass kicking-est moves ever and he somehow was managing to maintain some tenet of self control. I was a little insulted.

104

"You're different."

His first words in weeks almost put me right back on the floor where he left me last time. But not out of fear or trauma; I had simply forgotten how rough, deep, and seductive his voice was. And his comment sounded...worried? It took everything I had not to falter, but I wasn't about to give in so early in the game. No. He wanted fleeting pleasure just like everyone else here and he was damn well going to get it.

I ignored his commentary and ran my fingers through my hair as I bent backwards away from the pole, willing my groin into the cold, hard metal. He remained silent again for what seemed an eternity. I started to wonder if he was even there.

And then he said it. The worst thing possible. The only words that could possibly have thrown me back into the mind-fuck I was trying desperately to get out of.

"I was worried about you."

No, my mind was raging. *That's not how this is supposed to work. There's no fucking worry here. You don't care fuck-all about me, remember?*

I willed him. I willed him to take it back. I willed myself to forget it. I wrapped my legs around the pole and jumped into an acrobatic spin, nearly knocking him down in my wake. I heard him stand but I continued as if entirely unaware of his presence.

"Something's wrong," he said. And then, with a sincerity and care that would throw any natural girl into full-on orgasm, he stopped me, pulled my hand softly into his, and asked with an almost inaudible catch in his throat: "Are you okay?"

Fuck.

*   *   *   *   *

I remember that night like it was yesterday. She was different. I can't really explain how. Something just seemed...off.

I shouldn't have been there anyways. I should have stuck to my plan and stayed far, far away from that club. Far away from the place that could destroy my career. Far away from a sight that turned me into an aching, needing, fucking glowing piece of shit.

Far away from her.

Four weeks I had made it. Four measly weeks. It wasn't enough to bring me to forget her. I hated my goddamned lack of self control. I hated it almost as much as my publicist hated it.

"You can't go back there," she said, "you'll be done if they catch you."

Ha. Like I ever wanted to go there in the first place. Strip clubs weren't my scene. I'd never even stepped foot in one for God's sake. But that brother of mine – that piece of shit brother who came up with the "great" idea to distract me from my divorce – he fucked it all up. I was doing fine before he dragged me there. I was doing fine even after the throng of strippers started pawing at me and rubbing their sequins against me. But when I spotted her through the crowd, I knew I was done. I knew I'd be back.

And then when she danced on stage looking like sex incarnate...GOD...it had been a long time since I had gotten laid. I watched her every move, my eyes glued tightly to that hot ass even after she walked off-stage.

She caught me staring. *Yeah, baby, that's exactly what I want.*

I wanted her to see me scaling her, undressing her with my eyes. I looked hard for some essence of reciprocation. When she started giggling with her coworker and subtly eye-fucking me, I knew I had her.

I could have watched her forever. But I'd

106

already spent far too much time in that dump. The moment she walked off the stage and broke my trance, I ran out of the dump. Despite her feigned resistance to my charms, I knew if I didn't leave I'd ask her to dance for me, then make out with me in the alley, then join me in the backseat of my car.

I know; I'm an ass.

Running wasn't enough. I still couldn't get her out of my head. She'd had these quirky little looks that had me... entranced? God, that's so lame. She was hot, okay? She'd scrunch her little nose while she danced and her eyes were alight with pleasure, darting hysterically around the room as she walked off stage. I wanted her to look at me that way. I wanted her eyes to shine and her cute little nose to crinkle...it's one of the reasons I had to go back: I didn't get to watch her long enough. I had to have more. As soon as possible.

Good God, I am such a pussy.

I was such an idiot. I'd been so caught up reeling her into my game that I completely forgot all discretion. But whether or not she recognized me, when I waved that money in front of her boss's face upon my return for a second round of Navaeh, he had no interest in questions about my identity.

Good. Because I never should have come back in the first place. I never should've requested that private dance; that alluring dance that cemented my body to hers and made me feel more alive and fuck-ready than I ever have. Even with the blindfold, the whole situation was precarious – all it would take was one piece of fabric falling out of place…

Yet here I was. Again. A chump. Cursing myself for my lack of self control while simultaneously flying high just looking at her. She was sexier than ever as she sauntered in without a hint of the insecurity she used to hide behind. That was good, I guess. No sass this time, not a single word, in fact. It was strange. I just couldn't help but

107

think...maybe she seemed angry? Why would she be angry? I really didn't know but her face carried a fairly distinct scowl and it was difficult to determine if it was meant for her shady boss or for me.

I watched with caution at first, and then decided to approach her. "You're different."

Not the most intelligent start, but it was better than nothing. She didn't have much to say, though. She continued her dance, ignoring me with such fluidity that she almost knocked me over.

Yeah, she was pretty pissed.

I didn't know what to say. Or do. I didn't even know why she thought there was a reason to be angry with me. What the hell was I supposed to do? But I needed to connect with her somehow. Make her feel she could trust me.

Get those clothes off and get a good fuck.

At least that's what I told myself I was doing when I reached out for her hand and asked if she was okay. Once again, she didn't answer. Then back to the routine.

Since when do women not respond to my touch? What the fuck is wrong with her?

I sighed and turned to make my way back to my seat. The woman had spoken; this was all I was going to get for today. May as well enjoy the eye candy while I suffered through her silence.

But she wasn't done. In fact, she took me completely off guard by grabbing my arm and tugging me towards her. For a second my dick twitched because I thought she was going to pull me in for another dance, but that was pretty goddamned naive.

"Why the fuck are you here?" she seethed into my ear, her tone heavy and demanding. She wasn't teasing this time; she was pissed. "What do you want? And why do you keep coming back here and making me wear this stupid fucking blindfold?"

108

Okay, I guess I wasn't as bad at reading women as my ex-wife thought. I stood flustered. How the hell was I supposed to respond to those questions? I didn't know the answers; I was barely able to justify my return to myself.

I took a deep breath and decided to go with honesty mixed with a touch of manipulative flattery. My profession made me quite good at this.

"I wanted to see you," I said, surprising myself by gently pulling her closer. "I... I like..." I stumbled around like an idiot. *Real smooth, fucker.* "...I like watching you. I like the way you dance. You're very good." I could've shot myself. Jesus, this was getting better and better.

"I see," she responded coldly.

Not the response I was expecting in return for my complimentary words.

"Why don't you sit the fuck down then, and leave me alone." She let go of me and reached for the pole as if to continue the routine.

I stood stunned. I had not been talked to like that since...well, since I last spoke to my sister...

"You don't like talking to me?" I asked. It slipped out without my permission.

Pathetic. So fucking pathetic.

She seemed to consider my question. "I know what you're here for," she began, "I don't know what the blindfold is about, but whatever, let's get on with it. You'll get your money's worth."

Ouch. This chick had a stinger. "Fine," I threw my hands up in the air. "You keep dancing and I'll keep pretending that it's not driving me mad that I can't touch every fucking inch of you."

I didn't like the emotion that snuck into my voice at the end of that statement. I didn't like the statement altogether, actually, but my mouth seemed to be determined to run off without my consent.

I stole a glance in her direction. Did she believe it? Did *I* believe it? I mean, did I

109

actually believe I *didn't* really feel this way? Because the words radiated through me with a penchant of passion that took me by surprise.

I had to believe it, that this was all a ruse. That I was saying it just to get her under me so I could get her out of my system and move on with my life. I couldn't feel it – not for real. It was too risky, for her as much as for me.

Silence stretched on. It drove me mad. I needed a reaction. Did she feel the same way? Did she want me? Did she look forward to these messed up visits as much as I did? Or was I just a chump?

And then it hit me. This was my out. This was what I needed: I needed to know I was a chump and that she was just another shit-faced exotic dancer playing the fool. I just needed to get her to say it.

And so, I flung the nastiest, most insulting words I could find at her, a final attempt to put this whole situation to bed. "Let's see you work it, whore. I bet a cunt like you can give me more ass than that. Turn around so I can pretend I'm sucking your tits."

Silence.

And then I got what I wanted.

She came at me and shoved me up against the wall, her hands on my throat and her teeth clenched. She was stronger than I expected. I choked for air as I grappled with her hands, trying to rip them from their hold. I could feel my face flushing red, filling as if to burst.

Even as I stand here at the airport and watch her sit dejected and lost – but still as beautiful as ever – on the exact bench where I requested she meet me, I can't help but muse over one thought that runs through my mind like a broken record: I'm a fucking idiot to have thought this would work.

110

Chapter 13

I don't know what happened. I'd been insulted before. I'd been called all those words before, and worse. But not from him. I couldn't take it from him. A bomb went off inside me. A really fucking huge, fucking fucked up bomb.

Just like that I was choking him. I had him in my grasp, up against the wall, and I was ready to make him pay. He'd hurt me, teased me, and messed with my head. I wanted to destroy him the way I'd wanted to destroy the Pot.

"What the hell do you want?" I screamed again. "Who the fuck are you?" I started to shake. *What am I doing? This isn't the Pot! Get a grip, Ellie!*

I urged myself to calm down, but the reasonable side of my brain had lost all leverage. My strength started to wane and suddenly I was the one up against the wall, the cement cold and unforgiving. It chilled my bare skin to the bone. But not as much as the breath of this man on my face. He had my arms pinned to the wall, his pelvis holding my body, unmoving. I could hear Fred's

112

footsteps.

"Fred, no! Let me handle this mother-fucker!" I screamed. This wasn't going to end this way. If he was going to get his come-uppance, it was going to come from me.

"No ma'am!" Fred responded forcefully, "I have a job to do."

"Fred, no!" I screamed. I threw all my energy into escaping my prison, but I could hardly budge.

And then I did the worst thing. The worst possible thing I could do in a moment when all I needed was to feel powerful, strong, and in charge.

I started to cry.

No, I'm not talking about wussy, sniffley, little-house-on-the-prairie crying. I'm talking Niagara Falls, Hurricane Ivan, and a snotty green California mudslide all wrapped into one solitary man-deflecting display of emotion.

Fred's steps halted.

I could imagine the look of shock and uncertainty on his face. This hadn't been my aim; I'd simply run out of outlets. My knees weakened and I slowly sank to the floor. My beautiful stranger followed me down and wrapped me tightly in his arms.

"Fred, please," I whispered, "Just give me ten minutes."

Fred grunted, but I knew he wasn't going to get his hands dirty with the girly mess before him. He stalked off to the booth towards the back of the room, stepped in, and shut the door behind him.

I relaxed a little – very little. My entire body was taking part in my sobs, from the hiccups in my belly to the twitches in my toes. I took advantage of the cloth wrapped around my eyes and used it to dab away the unending tears that crashed unwelcome across my knees. I was tempted to remove it, but wasn't sure I could handle the stress of finding out who was sitting with me. I didn't

113

really care at that moment. I just wanted to cry and be held. I didn't give a damn who did the holding.

"I'm so sorry," my ball-capped stranger whispered, the stubble on his cheeks scratching softly against my forehead.

I shook my head. Why was he sorry? I was the one who attacked him. I was the one now crumpled in a heap on the floor.

"I don't know what happened. I've never spoken to a woman like that before. You're beautiful, you're amazing, you're..." he paused. "I know you want to know who I am. I wish I could tell you. Trust me, I want to tell you. So badly..."

I didn't want to do this right now. His confessions were only goading my tears. Flashbacks from that night with Mia crept back into my head. My breath caught and I started to panic.

No, Ellie, not now. You can't handle this right now. You can't go back there. It would be better to pass out again!

The beautiful stranger pulled me in closer.

"Please, tell me it gets better," I sobbed.

He let out a light-hearted snicker. "You mean life? You want me to lie to you? Because if so, there's a whole host of other topics we can discuss – good politicians, true religions, ethical wars..."

I giggled through my tears. It was the most I'd ever heard him speak and it was what I needed: a reminder that even in shitholes there are jokes to be made.

"Can I please take off this goddamn blindfold?" I pleaded between my half-sob-half-giggles. "I promise I won't look at you." I sounded so lame – like a ten-year-old begging for ten more minutes on the ipad.

I could feel his smile on my forehead. He released me momentarily, reached over my head, and slowly pulled the bandana off, catching a few gentle strokes of my hair along the way.

I buried my head in his chest.

114

"Your friend isn't going to come back over here, is he?" he asked nervously.

"No," I replied. "It's not unusual for girls to request he leave for certain 'special' guests. He won't bother us unless I ask him to."

"You've got a lot of power around here. Sounds like I'd better watch myself."

I giggled. "You have no idea."

"Oh, I've seen you on stage. I think I have a pretty good idea how much influence you have."

I sighed and sank deeper into his arms. It occurred to me that we hadn't really had any "normal" moments since we met. Our only contact had been these wordless kinky dances. And now here I was, making a huge scene out of my personal drama. And here he was, not leaving...

I should be the one asking him to wear the blindfold.

He started to sing a song. Some old song from the days of saloons and handmaidens, I would guess. He crooned away, his voice a gritty, raw baritone. It soothed me. I ran my hand up and down his arm, memorizing every muscle and vein, enjoying the comfort of his skin on mine.

"So, are you, like, ugly or something?" I blurted out after a few minutes of his flawless serenade. It would have been a great moment to be a turtle.

Luckily, he burst out laughing. "Is that why you think I use the blindfold?"

I paused. "I don't know. Maybe you're old? Or fat? Or really, really, really hairy?"

He laughed again and held my hand as he ran it up and down his arm another time or two. "Does that answer your question?"

I considered. "You could still be ugly. My hands won't tell me that."

He swallowed. "I am ugly." I tensed. He wasn't joking around. "Just not in the way you think."

115

Um, what the fuck was that supposed to mean? "So you blindfold me because you're afraid I'll see this...ugliness?" I tried to imagine a huge wart on his face, or a scorching case of acne. No, it just didn't seem to fit.

"You could say that," he concluded. He caressed my hair, twisting the ends around his forefinger.

"You're really not going to tell me anything useful, are you?" I meant to tease, but my frustration was hard to mask.

He was slow to respond and I began to wonder if I'd offended him. Of course, it would have been a hell of a lot easier to tell if I could *see him*.

He kissed my head, "I want to..."

I was too tired to argue. I knew that Randy would freak out if we stayed in there longer than the average time period of, say, two or three fucks so I pulled myself to my feet, careful to keep my eyes diverted. He stood up behind me and slipped the blindfold back across my eyes. He turned me around and stepped in. I could feel his face approaching mine...

"This is strictly a no-kiss zone," I hissed.

It was true. It was probably the only rule we actually maintained flawlessly. But I wasn't keeping it just to maintain my stripper integrity. In a small way, I wanted to punish him. Not a lot, just a little bit. Enough to get him back for stubbornly holding all the cards. Enough to make him feel like he wasn't going to get a free lunch out of this fucked up arrangement.

He squeezed my hand and turned to the door. I didn't want to be vulnerable, especially after drowning him in my lake of tears, but I couldn't help myself.

"Are you coming back?" I hated how hopeful I sounded. It made me want to barf.

He turned back and chuckled softly. "I don't

116

think I can help it."

*   *   *   *   *

It was almost sickening how cheerful I was the following week: dancing around the living room, singing songs, complimenting my boss...it was all so out of character, especially as of late. I even called up my sister-in-law to apologize and make dinner plans. I had to be tripping to do something that fucked up.

But none of it seemed to matter anymore. I felt too good to care about, well, much of anything. I got a lot of writing done before work – enough that I had completed eight chapters of my novel! I even wrote up a couple of query letters and researched some agents. I wasn't quite ready to jump in the deep end, but I was close enough to finishing that I wanted to be prepared. I got lost for a while in that daydream – the dream of being a published author. I could see myself at book signings, chatting with my enthusiastic fans. Someday I would get a movie deal and get to watch my stories play out on screen. I knew I had a lot of work to do to get there, but my good mood convinced me that maybe, just maybe, I might actually have a shot at the life I really wanted.

Work was better, too. My handsome stranger (hey, I can pretend, can't I?) came in every day that week. Well, every night. Every night I was working. Which was good, because I didn't want to have to dampen my good mood by beating the living shit out of any of the other girls who might jump him when I wasn't around to maintain my territory. I felt a bit lonely on my days off, but I made sure to keep myself occupied with writing and politics.

Friday night was the best night. It's always the best night for tips – nothing makes a man hornier than a hard week of work he hates

117

followed by a free night to himself. But this week, it was the best night because of him.

Each night things had gotten hotter and hotter. The first night, we did our usual sexy dance. The second, he slowly and gently slipped my top off, leaned me up against the pole, and let me make good work of it while he watched, copping a feel here and there. I was impressed he maintained that kind of control; I was about ready to rip his clothes off and fuck him right there. It seemed, though, that his unbending self control helped me keep my head straight; I liked that. The third night, he gave up all propriety and ran his hands over every inch of my body, licking his way up each leg and sucking on my belly button. Oh God, it was beyond erotic. Still not a kiss, still not a hand below the swimsuit line had passed between us but I was pulsating and sweating in ways I didn't know were possible.

I was shaking in my heels just imagining what this evening might have in store.

I waited anxiously for Randy to collect me. As always, my eyes were glued to the door in hopes of catching sight of my beautiful stranger, any of him. No such luck. He must've had some kind of secret entrance. I almost squealed when I felt Randy's fingers on my arm. I took off for our private room by the bar without even looking at him.

"Navaeh, wait!" Randy called, urgently.

What? For God's sake, I've been waiting for this all day! I stopped and tapped my right toe impatiently against the cement floor.

"You're going the wrong way," he implored.

Huh? Oh no, did someone else request a private dance? Am I going to miss my beautiful Stranger?

Randy, clearly irritated, gestured backwards towards the back of the club. Towards the Mud Room.

Oh.

118

For a moment I couldn't move. My adrenaline pumped wildly with the possibilities, but...but I'd never been in that room with him before. I mean, I'd been in there with plenty of other strange men, but...this was different. I didn't know how this would work. What if I couldn't please him? What if I got stage fright and left him with an orgasm-less stripper?

I swallowed the huge lump in my throat and meandered through dirty tables, chairs, and ass-grabbing clientele until I reached the Mud Room. I stood outside for a moment and observed the faded paint and splintering wood on the door. The frame had all sorts of heart-shaped graffiti penned into it from previously satisfied customers. Almost every girl in the club had her name up there – a trophy of sorts, I suppose. Would my Stranger be etching my name up there when we were done?

Something in me felt I would not leave this room the same woman I was going in.

A blindfold appeared over my eyes, tied in the back by Mia. "Let's go, chicka," she said and she followed me in.

"Mia? What –

She answered my question before I could finish. "Your buddy here wanted to be alone with you – no security. Randy said no and your friend threatened to take his business elsewhere. They compromised by agreeing that I will be your security. Your friend actually seemed more than happy with the arrangement..."

I was still confused. "But you're not wearing –

"I've already seen him before. I guess he figures I really don't know who he is. Not that I'd give a damn anyways."

I wanted to protest being the only one left in the dark, but as soft sultry music began playing, I knew I was up to the plate. Mia guided me to his

119

chair where he stood and he pulled me in for a deep and handsy hug.

"I missed you," he breathed.

I giggled. "It's only been one day."

He inhaled deeply. "It feels like much longer."

He stepped back and sat down, leaving me to my vulnerable blindness. I started with my hands in my hair – I knew he liked that. Within moments my black skirt was sliding slowly down my thighs and to the floor. I turned around to kick it aside, leaning my near-bare backside towards this unknown man who made me crazy. He traced the ties of my bottoms across my thigh with one hand. I leaned in to his touch, memorizing the warmth and roughness of his fingers. His other hand reached for my other thigh, brushing my skin up to my waist and causing me to shudder. I rolled my hips around and around, each time moving a fraction of an inch closer to him. His hands followed my movements, moving up and down between my thighs and my belly button. I felt his lips kiss my lower back.

I froze.

"Sorry," he said, "I forgot the rules for a second."

He pushed my hips to the side to restart my sensual act and I followed suit. Rules or no rules, that may have been the hottest kiss I'd ever experienced.

His hands crept slowly back up my sides to the base of my breasts. Yesterday's massacre had been beyond blissful and I was anxious to repeat the experience, too. As his fingers reached the ties at the back of my top, he stopped.

"Mia," he said. His voice sounded raspy and sexier than I remembered. "You take it off."

Holy shit. Really?

I turned in the direction I'd left Mia. She wasn't far. She turned me around, placed her hand

120

on my pelvis to pull me close, and rolled her hips with mine as her other hand worked to unfasten my top. She knew exactly what he wanted.

My top fell to the floor and we continued our libidinous duet, giggling softly before switching sides so I could remove her top as well.

I didn't have the sense of mind to think of it at the time, but in retrospect, I'm quite certain Randy's net worth doubled in that moment alone.

Mia turned me back around and her hands escaped up across my belly to fondle my breasts and she nipped and kissed my back while grinding into me from behind. Oh god, her hands felt amazing. Something seemed distinctly different about her. She was getting into this more than usual; she was enjoying it! It occurred to me that she might have been wanting to do this for a while. The fervor with which she ravaged my body confirmed my suspicions. She turned me around again and, hard and fast, her lips were on mine, her tongue exploring my mouth, her fingers kneading at my nipples. I pulled her in close, returning her passion and feeling my pulse quicken as I leveraged my thigh between her legs, grasping her ass with one hand and sneaking my thumb over the top of her breast. She gasped. Her leg wedged easily between mine and we started moving together. Up and down we moved, torturing each other with a massage I felt quite certain was beyond our wildest dreams.

I'd never been so turned on by a woman before. Maybe it was because it was Mia and I loved her dearly, but as much as I appreciated the female form, I had never wanted it like I did in that moment. I pulled her hair hard, licking her neck and wishing I could see my handsome Stranger wriggling and panting in his chair.

That's what it was. That's what had me so hot and bothered. The idea that he was watching me, enjoying a moment of rare girl-on-girl ecstasy –

121

that's what had me tied up in orgasmic knots. I pictured his eyes scaling our bodies, watching our pussies rubbing each other while goose bumps spread across our arms and sweat trickled down our legs.

I leaned down to wrap my lips around Mia's rock hard nipple. She gasped as she tipped over the edge of ecstasy, crying out and pushing harder against me to belabor the moment. Her outcry tipped me off and I came equally as hard, sucking deeper on her breast and shivering at the sensations her fingers left trailing across my chest. I squeezed my legs tightly together, rubbing harder, deeper, savoring the feeling of her between them. We continued to pulsate together until I heard a moan from the chair next to me. The sound was so succulent and deep, it drove me to the cusp of a second orgasm, this one prepping to be more intense than the first.

I pulled away from my sweaty, panting friend, pulled her behind me, and faltered forward until I was straddling my stranger. I could feel his dick poking up hard underneath his pants as I recklessly grabbed his hand and shoved it between my legs. Mia sat behind me, her tits lightly caressing me from behind as she continued her sensual massage of my breasts, my back, and my neck. I could hear my stranger's breath deepen. He dove beneath my panties, rubbing hard as he sucked at my nipples. I rocked back and forth with his touch, screeching and sighing.

"Come on baby," Mia whispered from behind me, "One more…"

I came for a second time. This time in tandem with my Stranger, his fingers inside me, his hand pulling me close at the small of my back, and Mia licking my earlobes and kneading my breasts. The intensity of his orgasmic spasm drove me over the roof.

I died. I truly died in that moment. I

122

collapsed on my stranger, sated and exhausted. Mia smirked as she stood to give us a moment alone. He held me close, daring a kiss of my neck, my head, and my shoulder. The rules suddenly had no meaning.

"God, you're amazing," he whispered.

Chapter 14

Low tips didn't bother me, annoying coworkers didn't bother me, even judgmental family members were easy to ignore after that evening of ecstasy. Five nights. It had been five nights in a row of licking, fondling, and feeling in a million different ways. It was hard to wish I knew who he was as the kinkiness of being blindfolded grew on me. There was nothing to focus on but my body and his hands. Those rough but gentle, sensual hands. We had pretty much done it all – well, all except kissing. And fucking. We hadn't technically fucked yet. I wasn't sure which I wanted more: the sweet confirmation of committed love that came with a kiss, or the solidifying bond that would accompany the ecstasy of feeling him inside me.

Either way, I was on cloud nine – happier than I'd ever been before.

In fact, I was so lost in the joy of my affair that I nonchalantly agreed to go to the amusement park with my family the following weekend. Why

124

do I always do such stupid things when I'm happy?

Can I just mention what a great audience you've been so far? I mean, unless you're doing this for a book report – and I highly doubt that – that means you're actually reading this because you enjoy it. Which is just baffling. I'm mean, I'm sure you didn't wake up this morning and say to yourself, "I've really been hoping to find a good story about a fucked up stripper who blind dances for an equally fucked up and potentially hideous-looking rich dude."

I'm just saying you're cool.

Ok, maybe I'm also saying this because things are about to go down the shitter. Again. And you're going to want to throw this book – or maybe me – out the window. Again. Think you can handle it?

Ok, bitches, your funeral. I'm just going to get myself all nice and comfortable here on my lonely bench because I can't say I'm too anxious to retell the rest of this story. I'd be happy to end it right there, on a high note. So hang on a moment, I'm just going to measure the distance between me and a stiff drink...

Ten paces. Good. Let's do this.

Mom and Dad wanted me to meet them at the nearby park before meeting up with the rest of the family. I figured it was their way of roping me into a lecture under the pretense of a nice morning in the sun.

Turns out I was wrong. What they had in mind was much worse.

The park was packed when I arrived, so much that I had a hard time finding a parking spot. After hoofing it all the way to the outdoor amphitheater, I was already pretty frustrated and not at all prepared for what I was about to experience. The amphitheater was packed. It took a good ten minutes to find my parents amongst the over-excited and fairly boisterous crowd.

125

"Ellie! Over here!"

I caught sight of my dad's bright red "I Love Paris" jacket over by a small clump of trees at the rear of the crowd. I jogged awkwardly in my flip-flops to join them, my curiosity piqued – had they brought me to a concert? I never imagined my parents to be the concert type but maybe the Osmond's were in town?

I gave my mom a hug and my daddy a kiss. "Quite the crowd here. What's going on?"

"Just wait. You'll see," my dad said with a grin.

"Cliff, it's about to start!" I'd never seen my mom so giddy.

Momentarily, my vision was overcome with visions of red, white, and blue. Everywhere I looked signs, banners, and flags were being raised in tandem with deafening cheers. On almost every sign was presented the name "Smith Anderson."

God fucking damnit.

The crowd was cheering mercilessly as the brown-haired man stepped up on stage, waving like a Miss America contestant. He stopped to shake some hands (Jesus, you're not Bono, dude) and blow some kisses to the crowd (or Shirley Temple, for that matter).

"Thank you, everyone. Thank you!" Anderson took center stage in his ridiculously expensive suit and even more ridiculous grin. "I appreciate all of you being here. This is a major election year and there are a lot of improvements to be made."

I glared at my parents who continued watching in awe. They couldn't just leave this alone, could they?

Anderson launched into a long-winded speech about all the life-changing initiatives he was going to implement. I couldn't help but roll my eyes every time he claimed he was the only one who could really bring about the kind of change we

126

needed. I was so sick of hearing politicians of any party make that empty promise. Nothing ever changed, and if it did, it was usually because someone got paid big. I was impressed, though, that he at least broached the subject of women's issues – workplace sexual harassment, equal pay, abortion – he hadn't a single useful thought about any of them but I had to give him credit for at least having those items on his radar.

"I know that with time we'll be able to bring Planned Parenthood down and abolish abortion for good."

I wanted to puke. *Seriously?* As if this motherfucker had any clue what he was talking about. The crowd went wild and I found myself feeling depressed about the company I was keeping. These people would follow this man to the grave – would they do the same if he were a woman? I scoffed. Not likely. Unless she was perfect and beautiful, of course. And had no libido.

His speech finally drew to a close and I heaved a huge sigh of relief. "Can we get the hell out of here now?" My eyes threw daggers.

Without a word, my dad grabbed my hand and dragged me through the crowd towards the stage. "Dad, what the –

As we drew closer and closer to the front, I could see he was making a beeline for the route Anderson was taking on his way out. Leave it up to Dad to think that a handshake with a lost politician would be enough to convert me to his way of thinking.

We reached the line of admirers just as Anderson was approaching the end. My dad made a huge show of getting his attention.

"Anderson! Anderson!" he called. "I'm a huge supporter of yours, I think you have great potential."

A few moments later, Anderson turned to him and flashed a charismatic grin. "Thanks, I very

127

much appreciate your support." He winked at a female supporter nearby.

Wow, he was much better looking close up. I felt myself flush as I stood awkwardly by my father's side.

"Maybe you can help my daughter." Good God, leave it to my dad to make me sound like a crippled horse. "She's a supporter of Boswell but I think there's still hope for her."

Anderson looked me over, his eyes widening in shock. He almost looked scared. *Ha! Never actually met someone from the other side of the aisle, eh?*

He recuperated quickly, cleared his throat, and reached for my hand in a much more formal fashion. "Nice to meet you..."

"Ellie," my dad said.

"Ellie," Anderson seemed to be trying my name out for size, "I wasn't expecting that."

What the fuck does that mean? I scowled. "What exactly were you expecting?"

"I don't know..." He was lost in thought.

I raised my eyebrows in expectation – the fans around me were starting to get impatient.

He snapped to attention. "Did you enjoy my speech?"

Never one to let a pretty face get in the way of standing up for my ethics, I regained my confidence. "Not really. But I don't really support politicians in general, so don't take it personally."

My dad frowned at my cheekiness. I ignored him and stared Anderson in the eye.

His eyes moved to the right side of my face and a look of confusion overcame him.

"Oh my God..." he murmured. He reached for my face.

I stepped back and vehemently smacked his hand out of the way. "What the hell do you think you're doing, dickhead?"

He looked like a deer caught in the

128

headlights, "I'm sorry, I uh..."

"Feel free to take *this* personally, fucker," I spat.

I stormed off, my dad at my heels, no doubt raging over my display of disrespect. He tried to stop me as I shoved my way through the crowd, but I evaded him. I was going to the goddamn amusement park. Now. This shit was over.

Chapter 15

I hadn't been to an amusement park in ages – I mean, *ages*. I think I was sixteen years old the last time I even dared a glance at a Ferris Wheel, and I only looked because I was driving down the highway and it happened to be looming behind a convertible with a ridiculously hot guy in the driver's seat (it was totally worth it).

See, sometime after I hit puberty, I developed an incredibly weak stomach (as you may have noticed). I couldn't do roller coasters anymore and I definitely, definitely could not do any sort of contraption that involved spinning. I could barely handle spinning the jewelry dolly at the department store. I know, it makes no sense – I spin around on the pole all the time. But it's different when I'm in control. I can decide how fast or slow I go and when I stop. There's no mechanical death trap whirling me around into the depths of uncontrollable insanity.

Luckily, the small town I grew up in outside Vegas didn't have an amusement park in the first

130

place so it was pretty easy to avoid. But since I'd moved near the city, I'd occasionally catch a glance of the through the trees after an afternoon downtown.

It was as foreboding as I remembered. But hey, I wasn't a child anymore. Jenny's kids wouldn't expect adults to go on rides with them, right?

Wrong.

In fact, it appeared that aunties in particular have the very special role of being the *one* person their nieces and nephews *insist* on taking on the roller coasters.

I walked through the park gate, which was basically just a couple of shoddy buildings separated by a turnstile, and immediately found my family. Kendra came running towards me with all the ardor of an eighteen-year-old cheerleader at her shotgun wedding, whipping me into a massive hug. I honestly did not know Kendra was so adventurous. Jenny gave me a knowing smile followed by a pat on the back from Tommy. Immediately I knew they had already planned my demise: I was to be Kendra's amusement park BFF for the day. I rolled my eyes as I hugged Mom and Dad and then turned to my bouncing niece.

"Ok, Kendra, I have a very special job for you."

She stood erect, to await her instructions.

"Your job is to find a large popcorn bucket – an empty one – and then hold it for Auntie Ellie while she pukes everywhere after every ride."

She glared at me. "No puking, Auntie Ellie! Mommy and Daddy said you're not allowed!"

It was my turn to glare. They had prepped her well. With Kendra's hand in mine, we ran (erm, she dragged me) off into the sticky, dirty, germ-infested junkyard they called an amusement park.

Kendra took me everywhere. She made me go on every ride. My family watched with wide

131

smiles as I stumbled off each one, green as grass, begging Kendra for a break.

"No breaks, no breaks!" she'd cry. "We won't get to all the rides!"

"I thought this was supposed to be a family day," I groaned to my parents. "Doesn't that mean you guys have to spend some time with her too?"

Mom smiled. "We have to watch little Tommy Junior."

My hand was just about to rise up, my middle finger extended, but before I could complete the motion, Kendra dragged me off again.

"God damnit!" My voice was getting hoarse.

"No bad words, Auntie Ellie, you'll make God mad!"

The roller coaster. The Ferris wheel. The Tower of Death. The Loop-the-Loop. We did them all. One right after the other. I felt a small spark of pride – I hadn't thrown up yet. That was worth something.

Right?

Dusk fell as I crawled towards the last ride of the day: The Tilt-a-Whirl.

I could feel the grease from my lunchtime pizza curdle in my stomach. "Kendra, I don't know..."

"Come on, Aunt Ellie, it's the last one!" She jumped up and down as she pleaded, "Pleeeeeeeeeeease!"

"Kendra, I'm exhausted. You might have to carry me home on a stretcher if I go on this one."

Her bottom lip extended into a grumpy pout.

"So Bill," my mom started, casually, but loud enough for me to hear, "What do you think of all the initiatives Smith Anderson is bringing to the table for the Republican Party?"

Dad looked at her in confusion at first, but her look of derision clued him in to her plan. "Oh! Oh, yes! Anderson is amazing. Boswell is taking

132

quite a hit in the polls."

Oh God, they know how to hit where it hurts.

But I still hesitated. Political bullshit was nothing against the spinning behemoth before me.

"Anderson may even have a chance to influence the reversal of Roe v Wade if he continues in this direction…"

My blood boiled. Dad knew exactly what he was doing, the rat bastard. I didn't want him to win, but I knew I was in no shape to take on this argument at the moment; hell, I could barely think straight.

Reluctantly, I threw my arm over Kendra's shoulder and with chagrin exclaimed, "Carry me to the Tilt-a-Whirl, lil' lady!"

She screamed. Right in my ear.

Ouch.

The line was irritatingly short and within a few nanoseconds, the teenage prison operator was securing us under a very questionable-looking metal bar.

My nerves quivered. "Are you sure this will keep us in? It doesn't look secure to me. Maybe we shouldn't ride this one, Kendra."

Kendra glowered and threw her body over the bar. "The bar stays!"

God, she's a brat sometimes.

I could feel the walls closing in as the ride began to move. We tilted backwards, gaining an altogether unsettling view of the sky, and then we whirled.

And whirled.

And whirled.

And whirled.

Oh Lord Almighty, I'm going to be sick. I'm seriously going to be sick just thinking about this. I pick up my newspaper and hold it over my mouth as I rush to the nearest trash.

I told you I have a weak stomach! Why, for the love of Jesus, did you think you'd enjoy this

133

story? I hate you.

Luckily most of the alcohol I imbibed in earlier has digested so I'm spared the embarrassment of detailing the contents of my dinner to you. Not that you don't deserve it. I'm just going to skip right past the whole Tilt-a-Whirl thing now, cool?

No? Get over it. I whirled; I puked. End of story.

Kendra wasn't too happy with me after my little scene that left three ride operators on a date with a bucket of soapy water, but my family thought it was hilarious. I sat down in the dirt just outside the entrance gate and tried to pull my head together. Tommy and my parents were laughing, Kendra was crying, Jenny was caught somewhere in between... The chaos was making my head hurt.

To the right of all this malarkey was a hot dog stand getting ready to shut down for the night. I focused my eyes on the vendor's hat to try to bring my brain back into focus. It was black cloth, flopped casually to one side, and sized just a tad too small for his massive noggin.

Without warning, light flashed in front of the hot dog stand and the vendor fell backward. A fire burned bright on the grill, searing the remaining hot dogs into tiny little black lumps of coal. The flames overtook my vision. They drew me in, beckoned at me. The smell of burning hot dogs flooded my senses. It wasn't a pleasant smell; it was...it was....

I clenched my head in my hands as the memory came into view. The fire. The burning. The smell.

The Pot.

He had been lying there in the trashcan outside the club. Mia and I had hauled him in there to rot with the rest of the garbage. His body was so cold. So...dead.

I groaned as the remaining memories of that

134

disgusting night so long ago rushed over me like a torrent.

"Come on, we have to get rid of the body," Mia stressed.

I could hardly hear Mia and I definitely couldn'tacknowledge her presence. I was completely focused on the body before me; hate, angst, and murderous rage surged through me like deadly poison. I only wanted one thing in that moment: to destroy him.

I had reached in my purse and, to my surprise, bypassed my gun and instead gripped my fingers over the wooden handle of my pocket knife, flipping it open as my skin turned cold and my decision became resolute. I rushed forward, my pocketknife raised high, and plunged it into the Pot's belly.

"Such a pretty face…" The words from nowhere haunted me.

Over and over and over I stabbed him, sickening cries coming from my parched throat.

"Such soft skin…"

When his belly lay bloody and gaping before me, I moved to his face, striking again with vehement force.

"So perfectly sexy for such a young girl…"

I had stabbed the living hell out of the man until he was nothing but an unrecognizable pile of flesh and I, a broken, sobbing, tormented demon of a woman.

Mia finally came to me, pulled me away from what remained of his body, and held me close. The blood of the Pot splattered across my clothing seeped onto her skin.

"Ellie! Ellie, what the fuck are you doing? For God's sake, you're fucking this whole thing up." She hugged me tight, removed the knife from my hand, and sat panting next to me.

I was spent. I didn't know what to do next. I couldn't think. My emotional tirade had caused all

135

my executive functions to shut down; only my ability to take orders was left. I looked innocently up at Mia.

"It's okay, we can still take care of this. The lighter. The one in Randy's office – go get it."

I rose to my feet and turned to the door, but couldn't remember how to get in. Mia shoved me aside, pulled the keys from her pocket, and rushed the building leaving me a dazed and blood-soaked mess. She re-emerged with a lighter and a gas can.

"Are you going to help me?" she shrieked, her voice becoming ever more stressed.

I didn't think. I couldn't think. I needed an order. I needed her to tell me exactly what to do.

Even lying there in the dirt of the amusement park, staring at that hot dog fire, I knew where this was going. I didn't want to remember any more. I had already seen myself at my worst. I wanted to stop the visions right there; I didn't want to know how debased I could become. *Go to sleep, Ellie. Pass out. I don't care; just stop the memories!*

I couldn't. My brain had been wrestling for weeks to bring this back and it had started down a dark path of no return.

I watched the scene play out in front of my mind's eye:

Together we hauled what was left of the body into the massive trashcan. Mia commanded me to grab the gas can and shook its contents all over the Pot and the surrounding trash. I complied without question. As I went to drop the can inside, I tripped on a parking stump and tumbled straight into the side of the heavy industrial metal garbage can, head first.

I remembered how badly it hurt. Mia ran to my side and checked my head while I cringed.

"It's just a bump and a cut," she said. "Do you have a first-aid kit in your car?"

I nodded. I stood up.

136

"Hold on! Give yourself a rest!"

I shut her up with an evil glare. I couldn't sit and I wouldn't sit. I had to do. Do something. Anything.

"Take off your clothes. Throw them in the trash can."

I got undressed and threw my clothing, Mia's clothing, the pocketknife, and the gun onto the fume-soaked body. Mia dropped the flaming lighter in and we both jumped back with the whoosh of heat. Then we stared, naked, wide-eyed, and afraid as the flames curdled around the Pot's body, suckling up his skin and perfuming the air with that rank melting odor I'd been smelling for weeks.

I watched. Like a criminal, I watched the body melt and drip down into the trash. I watched the man I despised become less than nothing – a figment of reality and a construct of my imagination. I saw his eyes bulge until they exploded. I watched his body turn black and his weight deplete until I could see nothing but ashen bones and his steel-toed shoes beneath the fire. And I liked it. I breathed in every moment of it.

And then, out of nowhere, Mia kissed me. She kissed me hard and passionately. I could taste her lipstick in my mouth while the burning flesh infiltrated my nose. She was turned on. This whole ordeal made her horny. And even worse: it made me horny too.

Holy fuck, we had sex! Right there. Right in that mucky, putrid, bloodstained cement. It was the most fucked up, desperate, emotionless, and passionless sex I'd ever had. No wonder I had such a hard time remembering it – I hadn't felt a thing.

A single tear fell to the dusty asphalt of the amusement park. A mix of shame, fear, and internal contempt overcame me. I couldn't handle it. I couldn't believe what I had done. I couldn't live with it.

137

I had to keep this criminal secret to myself. No one could know.

My body wretched and I turned over to release my demons into the dust once again.

Chapter 16

Chapter 13: Freedom. This was what freedom felt like – at least for a moment. For one second in time, she basked in the fullness of her senses and the absence of her worries. Number sixteen. Number sixteen was gone; only three left. Her time was running out – she could feel it – but she couldn't deny the sense of power and passion that encompassed her every time she got one step closer to her goal. The murderers, the rapists, the dung of the earth that hid underneath the sharp rocks of other peoples' sacrifices…they'd soon be gone. And she would be truly free. That one moment would last forever and life would glow with the flame of a million tiny gold rings.

She reached to her throat to feel the welts that never left. She dared a glance at her wrists where the scars would never fade. She stared with rage at the body before her that would never truly be gone, but would continue to haunt her until she completed her mission. That was the true journey: to quiet the ghosts, evict the evil, and fly listlessly into the winds of stolen passions regained.

139

I took the next few days of work off. I had to. I wasn't even sure I would be going back. I had a sudden urge to pack my bags and flee to Mexico. Or Bermuda. Or anywhere, really. I was a zombie; a total mess. If I even stepped foot into that club I was sure I'd be fired or, even worse, crowded on all sides by clamoring strippers, all hemming and hawing over me, begging to know what was wrong, dying to get some good gossip. No, I couldn't do that. I would just dissipate into the air right then and there.

I didn't deserve their empathy.

My psyche urged me to wonder what my beautiful stranger would do when he found me gone. But I couldn't bring myself to go there. I couldn't find the self esteem to care whether I lived or died, much less whether or not I found love. Or love found me, for that matter.

I didn't eat for days. A cheerio here, a slice of bread there.... that's all I could manage. My body was weakening. My muscles were dissipating. My interest in anything and everything had floated away with the stars that shined over the Tilt-a-Whirl. I stared blankly at the TV. The minute distraction of the colors dancing on the screen gave me the only ounce of peace I could muster.

I slept a few hours at night. Restless hours full of nightmares and pity parties and angry strangers yelling at me for being a murderer, a fucked up murderer who likes to get hot and horny to the smell of burning guts. It was all just too much. Too much all at once.

Randy called. Mia called, too. I didn't answer. I didn't even listen to their voicemails. I didn't even touch my goddamn phone. Leaving the house was definitely out of the question; too many people out there. Good people. Better people. I turned my little townhome into my own personal prison, torturing myself with the best and most

140

effective weapon I had at my disposal: me.

Almost five days had passed since the incident and I was lying on the floor in the front room, trying to ignore the TV. I sucked my breakfast shake – er, my dinner – through a straw, trying hard to keep it down while the news droned on and on. The topic trended to the sex trade and I couldn't resist gluing my eyes to the TV as various politicians spoke about sex trafficking and prostitution in Vegas. I turned the volume up.

"This is a real issue here. Everyone seems to think sex trafficking only happens in third world countries but it's alive and well here in Vegas and strongly tied to prostitution," the host began.

One of the Republican panelists spoke next, "Look, until we get our hands dirty and start arresting prostitutes, this problem isn't going away. We need to hunt down these criminals and hold them accountable."

Another panelist continued, "We have a huge outcry against abortion in this country right now. Until we look at these women and men who are involved in this trade and exact punishment, we will continue to not only harm the children being trafficked, but we'll continue to see abortion numbers rise."

The host interrupted, "And you really believe that outlawing abortion is the way to end this?"

"Yes," the politician responded.

I felt my blood begin to boil.

"Until we give them no other way out, these practices will continue. The only way to turn things around is to leave pimps and prostitutes with the responsibility for the human beings that they irresponsibly bring into this world. Make them live with their mistakes."

I stood up, grabbed my stone elephant decoration from the coffee table and heaved it at the television. The screen dented and cracked with a satisfying crash. I stared at the warped screen, happy to see the distorted faces of the people who wished to destroy the lives of young girls everywhere. I collapsed back on the couch in a fit, crossed my arms over my chest, and shut my eyes. I drifted off to restless sleep momentarily.

I was awoken by a knock on the door. When I opened my eyes, I saw nothing but a very confusing shade of red. I jolted to my feet in fear that I had spilled the blood of yet another innocent human being when I realized it was just my drink – the Bloody Mary from the night before, teetering on the edge of the coffee table. The fourth Bloody Mary.

My head was throbbing. It was nice, actually, to have something to concentrate on other than my self-loathing. I considered bashing in my knee to add another layer of therapy. I walked to the door and opened it.

Fuck. Why did I do that?

One of the neighborhood boys was standing there, bright, shiny, and innocent. Maybe he would be my next kill. I imagined smacking myself in the face.

"I just wanted to know if I could get my ball," he asked nervously. "We accidentally hit it into your backyard."

I gestured for him to enter the house and he bounced through the doorway with a mix of glee and caution. *Crazy lady next door has finally lost her marbles!* I took a step outside and sat on the porch. The boy skitted right past me, excited to resume his game. They were playing baseball in the street, using each driveway as a base. I watched them run around, carefree and stripped of all worries. So easy for them. They should just be kids forever. A blue Jetta pulled up in from of my house.

Oh no. Tommy.

I bolted back inside. I couldn't let him see me like this. What was he doing here anyways?

142

Psycho-bitch wouldn't let him touch my house with a ten-foot pole. I ran into the kitchen and hid behind the fridge, but I already knew it was too late. He'd seen me. And even if he hadn't, I had left my car out front. Rookie mistake.

He knocked loudly on the door. "Ellie! I know you're in there! You know I'm not going away until you open up!"

I stifled my tears. I knew he wasn't messing around. He slept on the landing outside my door once when I was in college because I'd called him in a drunken stupor. I opened the door and turned immediately in the other direction. He grabbed my shoulder and spun me gently to face him. He glanced past me to the broken TV, his face falling.

"Ellie, what the fuck?" His voice was stern, but dripping with concern.

I lost it. For the second time in the past two months, I became a bawling blubbery mess in the arms of someone who held no fault for my state. Tommy walked me to the couch and sat me down. I flipped on iTunes in hopes that the sound of Paul Patson crooning might help calm me. He sung a soft lullaby about losing love and hating himself.

Why would Paul Patson hate himself? He makes amazing music and doesn't burn bodies on a whim after a rough night at work.

Tommy pulled me close and rocked me just like I used to rock him when he was little. "What the fuck is going on, Ellie?" he whispered. His concern was heartwarming. He still loved me, even after everything I'd done – so long as he didn't know, anyways. "Do I need to beat someone up?"

I mustered a weak laugh. "You know I'd just take care of that myself, Tom-Tom."

He smiled. I hadn't called him that since we were kids. This moment felt comfortingly similar. If only a bandage could make it all better.

He let me cry for a little while, but I knew him too well – he would want answers. He'd never

143

seen me this upset before and he wasn't going to leave without an explanation. I tried to give him something to go on, but I didn't know what to say. I couldn't tell him the truth, but I also couldn't find a way to sum up what had happened in a way he would understand.

I finally choked out some words. "I just. I did something. Something really, really awful. You would never talk to me again if you knew what it was. I can't live with it. I'm trying, but I just...I can't."

I braced myself for it: yelling, running, looks of horror...one of those had to be next on the menu.

Instead, he sat in silence for a moment. It was unusual for him.

I fidgeted. *It must be worse than I thought; he's so upset he can't even find the words to explain.*

"Does it have anything to do with…" he reached for my facial scar.

I ruthlessly batted his hand out of the way. "I don't know what you're talking about. You know how I feel about people touching my face."

He seemed somewhat relieved. "Look," he started, rubbing his eyes with his fist. I wondered how much he'd slept the night before. "Whatever you've done, it won't make me stop loving you or respecting you or thinking you're the best sister a guy could have."

I took a deep breath. Was it possible that he really meant it? He still didn't know what I did...

He seemed to hesitate, shifting uncomfortably in his seat. I sat forward, forgetting my insecurities momentarily. He glanced rapidly around the room. My intrigue at his sudden change in demeanor was hard to hide.

"And if you swear to God almighty you will never share with anyone what I'm about to tell you..." He paused again.

Does Tommy have secrets too?

144

"Whatever you've done, it can't be as bad as what Jenny has done."

My sobs made skid marks. I was all ears.

Chapter 17

"Pinky swear first."

Tommy had finished making a bowl of popcorn and we settled on the couch for what I hoped was Jenny-really-is-super-fucked-up-like-me-deep-down story time. Tommy nestled into my second-hand couch pillows and popped a kernel of piping hot popcorn in his mouth. He draped his hand behind me as he contemplated the first words of his unexpected confession. He looked very comfortable now; maybe even relieved. Maybe he was getting tired of keeping secrets, too.

In typical Tommy style, he cut straight to the chase. "Jenny used to run coke."

I almost spewed my popcorn all over his very sincere, very worried face.

He continued without flinching. "It was right after high school, before I met her. It took me two years to get her to open up about it. She was dumped twice before when her boyfriends found out and she swore she'd never tell anyone again."

I could understand that. But Jenny the coke

146

runner...I was starting to like her better already.

"She had to deal with some pretty shady people in some pretty shitty neighborhoods, but she was an addict at the time, so it was worth the fix."

He stared down into the popcorn bowl. I had the distinct feeling he was picturing his wife in that bowl – once a lone and innocent kernel, running with the wrong corns. Then one day, shocked right out of it by the grace of Jesus and catapulted into a full life of puffy, flavorful snackdom, smothered in butter, ranch seasoning, and beautiful children.

Meh, he's not that creative.

"Tommy?" I asked, prompting him to continue.

He snapped to attention. "Right, sorry. It's just so hard to imagine her that way sometimes. An eighteen-year-old girl running across the country with thirty-year-old men, drugged up beyond conscious reality half the time..." He ran his hand through his hair.

"It's ok, Tommy," I soothed. " Hell, most of the girls I work with do drugs almost every day. You know I have no judgment. In fact, I actually think I might have a chance at liking her now that I know this."

He forced a pitiful smile then straightened up and cleared his throat. "There was a meth lab in town she frequented – that old shabby house on fourth. Remember that one?"

"Oh my God, I knew it!" I cried. "We knew there was something fucked up going on there, remember? It was the only house in town we refused to trick-or-treat at."

Tommy nodded. "It was a common drop location so Jenny went there a lot. She spent the night there sometimes."

I shivered.

"But a few months in, she realized it wasn't

147

just a group of addicts living there." He stopped again, rubbing his hands on his knees.

Why did he keep doing this? It was driving me mad! "Tommy, what? Who was living there?"

"Are you sure you want me to tell you this? It's not exactly a happy story and I could end up divorced over it..."

"Oh, for fuck's sake, I'm not a little girl. If you can handle it, I can handle it."

He shoved a massive handful of popcorn in his mouth. "Fine." He shifted positions so he was facing the TV instead of me. "There was also a kid living there. Jenny said she thought she was about four. She never left the house. She was super skinny, like, starving. She hardly had any clothes and apparently her toys were old discarded meth lab stuff like beakers, tools, and scraps of paper. She had them stashed in the corner of her room. Jenny walked in her room one day and the little girl threw herself over them, breaking one of the beakers and cutting herself." He looked at me knowingly. "Jenny says she thinks she built an attachment to the toys to make up for a lack of attachment to humans." He trailed off as I continued to stare, captivated.

He grabbed another handful of popcorn. "Jenny and a couple of guys went over there one day to get hooked up with some coke. They arrived just after the police showed up to raid the place. They drove around back to get the drugs and the money out before the cops found it and the guy and the girl that lived there jumped out the back window with all the contraband. I guess the little girl jumped too, but they didn't wait for her." He paused again.

I suddenly couldn't breathe.

"They jumped in the car and left her there, struggling to keep up but too small to run fast enough. I'd like to think they forgot she was behind them, but..." Tommy's hands massaged his

148

forehead.

I didn't dare move. I was terrified; could this be going where I thought it was?

"The mother fuckers backed right over the little girl. Just mowed her down and split." His voice broke with the words. "Pieces of wussy fucking douche shit, they were."

Tommy's face was flaming red and a few tears welled up in his eyes. His veins protruded from his arms as he kneaded his palms. He was both terrifying and so, so broken at the same time. My sweet little Tommy. No wonder they loved their kids so much.

"Jenny tried to jump out of the car to help her but the driver sped off before she could get out the door." He sighed. "She said she cried for three weeks after that. She still can't get the image of that little girl out of her head. She sees her every time she looks at Kendra."

"But..." I stuttered. "But what could she possibly have done? The girl was probably already dead."

"That's what I said. But she says she could've helped her. She could have sat with her in her last few minutes of life. She could've made a difference if she'd just acted sooner." He laughed with derision. "Jenny, a coward – it's the most absurd thing I've ever heard. She's the strongest woman I know."

Wow. I'd never heard him talk about her this way before. I had been so busy judging her for her religiosity, I'd never taken the time to find out why he loved her. "Tommy... I'm sorry. I had no idea..."

"What, that Jenny deserves your respect?" he snapped. He shook his head. "Sorry, you don't need that. It's a two-way street with you two. But I didn't tell you that so you'd feel sorry for her; I told you because you need to get this idea that people expect you to be perfect out of your fucking head. I know you, Mom, and Dad have differences, but no one is hoping you'll sprout angel wings and fly straight to heaven."

I had to smile at the prospect. I felt so very far from angelic.

He continued. "I don't agree with Mom and Dad – and even Jenny – on hardly anything either. I don't even agree with you on everything. But I know the person you are and I know you're doing what's right for you. So give yourself a goddamned break."

I didn't know what to say. I wanted to believe him, I just didn't know how. Did I really think everyone expected perfection from me? I didn't really know. It would certainly explain all the tension between me and, well, anyone who didn't understand my decision to be a stripper. Which was a lot of people...

"It's harder than it sounds," I murmured.

"I know," he empathized. "Jenny still struggles with it too."

I raised my eyebrows in disbelief.

"Well," he huffed, "why do you think she's so fucking stuck on this religious kick? Do you think she thinks it's fun?"

Well...yeah...

"After she watched that little girl die, she went looking for something – anything – to get her out of that mess. Church was the first solution she found and she latched on tight. She knew she'd never make it out otherwise. And she's still hanging on, still hoping that someday she'll actually be forgiven for what she did."

He walked into the kitchen and returned with a beer in hand. "And God knows, I can't convince her. So I can only hope that someday God – whatever he or she is – will."

It made sense. A lot of sense. I was a little ashamed I hadn't picked up on it myself. But I'd knocked my shame quota out of the park so I decided to let this one slide.

"Does any of this help at all?" he asked. "Or did I just risk my entire marriage to present you with the screenplay for an R-rated movie?"

I had to laugh. "It helps. A lot, actually. Thank you."

He gave me a satisfied nod.

Tommy's pep talk wasn't a magical self-forgiveness medicine, but it did relax me enough to spend the next hour or two laughing with him over old memories. It felt so good to pass the time with my baby brother. Even as the clock ticked, I knew these few hours would not soon escape my memory. I was tempted to seek out a way to lock them up in a tiny box to preserve for eternity, but eventually it got late and Tommy had to get back to that ex-coke-running wife of his.

As I walked him to the door, something occurred to me. "Hey Tommy, how on earth did you know something was wrong with me?"

He smirked. "My spidey sense. Didn't you know I'm psychic?"

I crossed my arms over my chest.

"Okay, okay, don't get your g-string in a twist. Your boss called me."

My look of confusion augmented.

"Apparently I'm your emergency contact and you haven't shown up for work for a while."

Oh yeah. I'd forgotten about that. Poor Randy. Poor Mia! She must be frantic over what I must be doing (or saying).

Before he left, Tommy gave me one word of caution. "With Jenny..." he began. "I know you've learned a lot about her tonight but you can't change your attitude towards her too much, okay? She'll know I blabbed. You're going to have to peel off the bitchiness one layer at a time."

I smiled. "Aye aye, cap'n. Bitchiness still in tact, sir." I reached out for a hug and basked in the warmth of the last moment of peace I'd feel for

151

quite a long while – I could already sense the anxiety and guilt waiting impatiently at the door. *Like a couple of damn Jehovah's Witnesses.*

"Hey, Tommy."

He turned to look at me from the porch.

"Don't get any ideas. I'm still not going to your fucking church."

He laughed in the glow of the evening porch light. "I wish I could say the same."

Chapter 18

Everything was perfect after that. My talk with Tommy completely healed me and I was wistfully returned to the Ellie everyone had always known and loved.

Not.

Look, when you rub shit into the carpet, it doesn't come up the first time you put a soapy rag to the floor. It takes time, dedication, and a shit ton of really shitty days to even begin to patch things up. And even then the carpet is never quite the same.

I did eventually get back to work. But despite my relief at knowing that even Tommy's Jesus-loving, church-going, daughter-of-the-Lord-Almighty wife had some serious bruises in her past, I still couldn't forgive me mine. It was too fresh, too real, too unbelievable.

I had only missed about a week of work, but I was still fragile that Friday of my return. I found I had lost that confident edge I briefly gained

153

after the whole Pot incident. In fact, I had gone quite the opposite direction.

Randy gave me a mouthful from the get-go, raving on and on about our "special guest" who had been in every day begging to know when I'd be back and threatening to close the whole place down if he didn't get an explanation for my absence. The look of shock on Randy's face when I sidestepped my more recently utilized 'fight fire with fire' strategy and instead burst into flaming tears would've been worth several Academy Awards.

He pulled me into his office and leaned in close (mostly because it was a tiny office and there was barely enough room for two people). "Ellie, what is going on? Shit, I've never seen you like this before. Are you sure you want to come back?"

I looked at him in panic, "Randy, I have to come back. I can't stand another day sitting around my house. Please, I need to stay busy."

He seemed relieved. "Well, if you can afford to, let's keep you at the bar tonight, at least until your friend shows up." He paused and looked at me inquisitively. "Do you think you can handle him?"

I nodded, wiping my eyes and trying desperately to pull myself back together.

"Good," Randy said, and he returned to his demanding demeanor. I opened the door to leave, but Randy stopped me. "Ellie?"

I glanced back to find him fidgeting and shooting awkward glances around the room. I raised my eyebrows.

He sighed. "I was worried about you, okay? I've never been unable to get a hold of you before." He kicked a crumb across the floor. "I just... I'm glad you're back."

Vulnerable Randy. How about that? My heart exploded and my emotions followed suit. Tears poured down my face yet again and I hugged

154

him with deep gratitude. Once again, I had knocked him clean off his game and his nervousness elevated.

"No. No, don't cry! Please." He looked like a firefighter standing alone before a burning forest. He pulled away, grabbed the box of tissues from his desk, and started flinging them at me erratically. "I was just kidding! I wasn't worried about you, okay? I don't care. I-I don't even like you! I hate you! For God's sake, just stop crying!"

My tears exploded into laughter that bellowed deep and hearty. Oh goodness, it felt good to witness such excellent comedy in a moment piqued by so much unnecessary emotion. Randy stopped tossing tissues as I broke down into an all out guffaw, holding onto the doorframe for support as I collapsed to the floor. Tears still streaked my cheeks, but this time a broad smile accompanied them.

Randy looked a bit insulted and folded his arms across his chest in consternation. "Are you quite done?"

My giggles died down and I pulled myself to my feet, brushing off my skirt and wiping my eyes clear. I slapped my hand on Randy's shoulder and grinned. "Thanks Randy. I really, *really* needed that."

I returned to the bar – no need to try to temper the huge mass of awkward I had left in my wake. I could still see Randy standing inside his office door when I reached the counter, his face contorted and hands shoved firmly in his pockets. I spotted Mia making her way to her fallen soldier. Too much girl for him for one day – but Mia would make it all better.

My mood improved considerably. A few delightful customers came by the bar and I dropped my usual professional demeanor to have a couple shots with them. I laughed, I joked, I got a little tipsy. I got a lot more tips than usual.

155

I was cleaning up tables, singing along to the methodical clink of glasses as I loaded them onto a tray when Mia appeared by my side.

"Hey, chicka," she said. "Someone snuck in some contraband in the back. Wanna join me for a smoke?"

That sounded like the perfect compliment to my buzz. I nodded enthusiastically and followed her back to the dressing room. We snuggled up on the couch, nursing our much-needed joints. After a few puffs, I realized Mia was looking at me strangely. She almost looked...nervous? I'd never seen her nervous before – well, outside of the night with the Pot. But insecurity really wasn't her "thing". It popped into my head that she still might be worried about the whole Pot thing coming back to haunt us.

I sighed and rested my head on her shoulder. "Mia, would you quit looking at me like that? It's freaking me out. I haven't told anyone about the Pot, okay? I hardly even remember it." Well, that was massive lie, but it worked.

She looked surprised and laughed. "I'm not worried about that, Ellie. I trust you." She tucked a hair behind my ear.

I rested my arm on the couch behind her. "So what's the deal then? You look like you have something on your mind."

"It's nothing, I just...that blindfold guy – you're really into him?"

I snorted. "As much as I can be for someone I've never seen before and know absolutely nothing about." I took another puff.

"So...do you consider yourself taken right now? Or is this whole thing, ya know, casual?"

I turned to Mia in frustration. "Am I taken? God, Mia, are you trying to set me up with someone again? Because I'm really not in the mood. No, I'm not technically 'taken' but I'm not exactly looking to fuck one of Randy's buddies either."

156

Just then, Mia's eyes met mine with determination. I suddenly knew where this whole thing was going. Before I could protest, her lips were on mine, her hands in my hair, taking me completely off guard with her sudden unabashed expression. I kissed her back slowly – I loved her, after all. Just not in the way it appeared she wanted me to.

She pulled back and searched my eyes.

"Mia, I…" I didn't know what to say. How could I tell her? Was she in love with me? Would I be breaking her heart? "You're my best friend and I love you dearly, but…"

She winced and stood immediately. "It's no big deal, Ellie, I just figured it was worth a shot."

I looked at the door in confusion. "I thought you and Randy…"

"I do like Randy," she snapped. "It's just…you've always been special to me. And we've had some…moments. As much as I like how things are going with Randy, I just…had to know this first."

"I'm sorry, Mia."

She rolled her eyes. "Oh, fuck off, drama queen. Get back to work. I have an in with boss, remember?"

I smiled. I knew she was hurt, but she seemed just as anxious as I was to move past the awkward moment. I stood, doused my joint in the ashtray, and walked past her to the door.

"Ellie?" she said, stopping me. She sighed. "He's a lucky guy."

"*Who*, exactly?" I challenged with a willful grimace.

She looked me over with pity. "You know who. As much as you hate him, you love him too."

I bit my lip, pecked her on the cheek, and made my way back to the bar without a thought regarding my beautiful stranger. Love him or not, he was not an option.

157

I sighed as I weaved between the chairs and tables by the stage. The past few weeks had been bizarre and emotionally draining, but never in my entire life would I have anticipated that Mia had feelings for me. I dared a glance back toward the dressing room. Mia was quietly slipping into Randy's office and shutting the door.

Ah, a good office fuck. That ought to perk her right up. I smiled to myself and returned to the pile of dishes anxiously awaiting my magical touch.

As the soapy water filled the basin, a commotion broke out near the club entrance. Nothing terribly shocking, really, but a few raised voices and some scuffling was enough to draw my inebriated mind to attention. Randy went skedaddling past me, followed by a member of his security team.

I dumped my glasses into the hot water just as a group of four men went clamoring across the floor on the other side of the club, creating a rather Tasmanian Devil-worthy scene.

"Where is she? Where is she?" a voice screamed.

Oh God. Not Dashia's ex again. I watched as they dragged the man towards the back. Why were they dragging him into a private room? Just kick the bastard out!

I regarded softly the dishware in the sink. "Sorry, guys. You are shiny, utilitarian, and you make me a lot of money, but the little situation across the room is simply a whole lot more interesting right now." I pulled off my apron and ran to investigate.

I reached the closed door of the private room just as Randy exited. His face was a burning red with beads of sweat falling from his crooked chin.

He looked right at me. "Would you get in there and calm your fucking boyfriend down? He's drunk off his ass screaming about wanting to see

158

you and no matter how many times I tell him you're here, he just keeps shitting in my face!"

I blinked. "What? You mean the blindfold guy is in there?" My muscles tensed.

Randy nodded. "Yes! And he's a fucking mess." His face contorted in recollection of my breakdown just hours before. "Are you up for this? We can kick him out and tell him to come back tomorrow."

I shook my head. "No. You can't."

I rushed to his office, knocking over a few chairs along the way, grabbed the blindfold from his desk, and pulled it on just before I entered the private room. I walked in cautiously, unsure in what state I might find my beautiful stranger. I reminded myself where the emergency exits were.

As I shut the door, I was surprised to find the room was relatively quiet. "Hello?" I called.

"Navaeh! Oh my god, Navaeh. You're here! That dickhead was telling the truth for once!"

I heard some scuffling.

"Don't fucking move," Fred seethed.

"Let him go, Fred, it's okay," I ordered.

Nothing.

"I said, let him go. He wants me; I'm here. He won't fight anymore."

Still nothing.

"She's right," that familiar voice cooed. "Please, I'm done freaking out, okay? I've just had a few drinks..."

His speech was slurring – it was definitely more than a few drinks.

"Fred, come on, for God's sake. Take a break, will you?" I heard more movement, then the sound of footsteps walking past me towards the door.

"Do you want us to stay nearby?" Fred queried.

I shook my head. "I'll be fine."

He heaved a sigh and continued out the

159

door with his comrades. I relaxed just a tad, glad to have reduced my audience, but entirely unsure how to proceed with this shit-faced version of my dream man.

I decided to start by stating the obvious. "You're drunk."

"I've had a some…stuff..." he attempted to correct me.

"No," I continued defiantly, "you're drunk. Do you really think it's a good idea to show up here like this? Completely fucked up and making a huge scene? What the hell is wrong with you?"

I felt a little awkward, as if disciplining a child. But that's exactly what that crumpled man seemed like at the time and I wasn't feeling super patient in my own inebriated state.

"Where have you been? You okay?" he inquired.

I sighed. "Look, I don't know what's going on right now and I don't really know what you expect from me. I'm here. Are you here for a dance? Are you looking for counseling? Because I'm not really qualified to do that on any level, especially lately."

The last two words brought the outside back in – the empty lot outside of the club walls. The lot where I murdered someone and apparently enjoyed it so much that I fucked a girl for the first time in celebration. God, this was not a good subject to explore on a buzz.

He didn't respond. I'd love to say he had some kind of transparent facial expression or telling gesture but, oh yeah, *I couldn't see a fucking thing*.

"Look, just come back when you're feeling better. I'll be happy to take care of you then."

I turned to leave.

"No!" he cried, his voice weak and needy. "Please, I just... I had a shitty week. I...I need you."

What about your wife? I thought to myself. I

160

didn't know a single patron in this joint that didn't have some kind of steady, strained relationship they were here to escape. Surely he was no exception. But I bit my tongue. A shitty week? That was something I could understand.

"Where are you?" I asked as I shuffled in the direction I thought I'd heard his voice.

"Over here," he directed. "Just keep coming straight."

He wasn't far. I sat down on the floor beside him and leaned up against the pole.

"I'm sorry," he pouted, "I'm a mess. I just…I need you right now. I've needed you all week, but you weren't here. You left me. Why did you leave me?"

The alcohol on his breath was so potent I began to worry that the mood candles on the outer edges of the floor might be too close. He was babbling like a buffoon.

"I've had my own shitty week," I moaned.

He pulled my hand into his lap. "Tell me about it."

I laughed. "No. You'll never come back if I tell you, and frankly, you're paying my rent right now."

He laughed much longer than was necessary for my feeble and vaguely insulting joke. "My story is no better."

"Maybe we should just stick with not talking," I suggested. "I won't dance for you tonight because, well, look at you. You won't remember a moment of it and I'm not so poor that I'd take advantage of a severely drunk and depressed man. But I wouldn't be opposed to some physical comfort..."

He reached for my arm and pulled me in. I wrapped my arms around his chest while he enveloped me like a blanket and we just sat there. Minutes ticked by. I didn't dare move – I was more comfortable and peaceful than I'd been in a long

161

time.

"You know, I'm not so drunk that I couldn't appreciate a dance," he cajoled.

I smiled. "I'm not sure I can move you to your seat."

"I can take care of that." He released me and I heard some movement that I can only assume was him lying down and rolling away from the pole a few paces.

"Very clever, even for a drunk guy," I joked.

"It's the only movement I can manage right now."

I pulled myself to my feet – careful to avoid a head rush – and started some simple and basic moves.

He was very vocal that night. Lots of whoops and hollers, and, most enjoyable to me, lots of commentary.

"God you are sexy," he kept saying. That was his favorite line, often followed by "keep going, baby, I love it".

Goaded by his sensual words, I increased the intensity of my routine. I curved my body around the pole, goose bumps forming and blood rushing with every word that came from those lips.

"I want to fuck you so bad right now..."

I stopped in my tracks.

"Sorry," he said. "That was drunk me getting carried away."

But I wasn't upset. In fact, something about those words flipped a switch in my brain. I knew it was wrong; I knew it was a bad idea, but the overwhelming stress of life and the intensity of my desire to mask it took me over.

"Do it," I said softly.

"What?"

"Do it," I repeated. "Fuck me."

He was silent. Then in a low voice, "You know I can't do that, Nevaeh. I could get booted for life. And I need you too much..." The drunk in him

162

was still talking but it no longer mattered.

"I don't care. I want you to fuck me. Right here, right now, up against this pole."

"Navaeh..."

I could tell from his tone that he was going to be stubborn.

Fine. I'd have to convince him to change his mind.

Chapter 19

I returned to my routine, but this time I wasn't planning to execute any impressive moves. I swirled my hips around and rubbed my hands up my body to my hair.

"Oh god, yes baby..." he murmured.

Then I undid my top. But I didn't let it drop right away. I let it hang there, teasing him as I sucked on my finger.

"No, no..." he whispered, "don't stop..."

"Fuck me," I moaned.

No response.

Good; that's progress.

I released the strap of my top and rolled my back against the bar, extending my chest out so my bare nipples caught the cool air from the vent and perked up. I heard him release his breath slowly and erratically. I teased my breasts and pulled on my nipples. "Oh God, that feels so good..." I moaned.

I knew it was tearing him apart, and I loved it. He was going to be swelling blood red and I was going to be wetter than an Asian tsunami. My fingers crept downward slowly as my hips rolled under my touch. I paused just below my belly button.

"Good god you are evil," he said.

I let the moment sit for a second, drinking in every last droplet of the sexual tension. My fingers twitched. My ass constricted. His breath caught. My fingers dove hungrily beneath the fabric of my g-string.

I screamed. *Seriously, I screamed. I never scream.* But the sensations were too much; too good. Too necessary. I could hear my stranger panting heavily, his hands moving rhythmically in time with mine.

I was starting to feel desperate. "Fuck me. Please." I wanted his rock hard dick inside me, shoving into me, owning me. I wanted it so bad I didn't even care that I was begging. My fingers worked around my clit, than massaged around the soft and burning entrance to my vagina, then back to my clit. Back and forth, back and forth....

"I'm gonna come," I complained. "I want you inside me when I come."

"Goddamnit!" he cried. "You know I can't. It's not just you – my fucking reputation is on the line."

His fucking reputation. I laughed to myself. We'll see how much he cares about that bullshit.

And then I did it. The one thing I had never done in that club – not on the floor and not in a private room. I pulled my hand from my aching pussy and grasped the ties of my g-string on each side with my hands.

"Navaeh..." His words held warning but with a very strong hit of anticipation. He wanted this as badly as I did.

That gave me the final boost of courage.

My hands jerked outward and my g-string fell to the floor. There I was, completely buck

165

naked in front of a man I knew nothing about; and on whom I still had not had occasion to rest my eyes. It felt amazing. Freeing. I felt like I could fly straight to orgasm heaven – but I wanted him with me.

One hand on my breast and the other inside me, I dug in. Deep, rough, and sensual.

"Just fuck me," I growled. "I murdered someone for God's sake; I need a good fuck!" I could feel the pressure building. My body needed a release so very, very badly.

I was on the edge and just about ready to let myself go when he slammed me up against the pole. I could feel his swollen erection against my pelvis and it took all my self control to hold off blowing my top right then and there. His lips were on my neck as I heard the sound of his zipper, then the plastic wrap of a condom. He threw my hands above my head, grasping them tightly, and in a moment that felt like an eternity, he tore into me. Oh God, he filled me so savagely and beautifully. Heaven was waiting and I craved it like a drowning sailor. I thrust hard, forcing him deeper inside me, relishing the cascade of firecrackers that shot through every nerve and vein in my body. It was only him and me and the ecstasy, the pure wholeness and utter fulfillment of the moment.

"Fuck, I've been wanting you like this for so long," he roared. "You feel so good..."

I grasped his arms, exploring the nuances of his muscles with my fingers, and released another belabored moan. This one set him off. He came violently inside me so my back grated against the pole. It didn't hurt. It was hypnotic – I did this to him. I made him so randy that he threw all caution to the wind just to have one moment of carnal bliss with this hot woman that made him completely crazy.

As he launched into his fiery explosion his lips wrapped around my nipple and sucked,

166

sending me into my own explosive orgasm. I cried out even louder this time, blissful tears filling the wells of my eyes once again, but I didn't care. His cock filling me, his lips sucking hard, his chest heaving, his hands grasping tensely my back and my wrist... It was an eclipse I'd been waiting months for, and it was beyond the depths my imagination could excavate.

We collapsed in a state of exhaustion, tangled up in each other and unconcerned with the discomfort of the cold cement floor. Our chests heaved and our fingers continued to explore each other's bodies one libidinous inch at a time. He had stubble on his face – I'd never noticed stubble on him before. I stroked it with my hand. He responded in kind, and for the first time in my life, I didn't cringe at his touch. I let him run his fingers over my pain, caressing it, healing it.

"Nevaeh," he breathed, "How in God's name do you do this to me."

I smiled to myself. I liked having this effect on him. I liked that my kick-ass sex made him feel better. I loved that he had shown up here every single day I was gone and that he had driven himself into a drunken stupor in his attempt to find me. I loved that he...

Wait, loved?

Fuck.

The planet-sized weight of reality heaved itself senselessly onto my broken spirit. *Mia was right. I'm in love with him.* It was time to face the music. I needed to know who he was.

I sat up. I figured this wasn't going to go well, but my battered soul couldn't bear anymore burdens; and being in love with someone I'd never seen was an amazingly gargantuan load to haul. I didn't want to scare him so I decided against the easy way out – simply removing the blindfold – and instead ran my fingers through his bushy hair and said softly, "I need to know who you are."

167

He stiffened. And definitely not in the good way.

"Please," I pleaded. "Let me take this blindfold off. I can't stand not knowing who you are. I...I like you too much." Fuck, what if I was completely alone in my infatuation? I couldn't risk it; I had to know who he was first.

He sat up.

I imagined he was at least considering my suggestion. "You must know you can trust me by now..." It was more a question than a statement, but not enough to garner a response. "I've told you some really shitty things I've done – one of which I dropped on you like an a-bomb tonight – but you're still here. That must mean something. The least you can do is let me see you."

"It's not that simple." His words were almost inaudible.

"It can be," I suggested.

"No," he snapped. "It can't." He paused. "You wouldn't understand."

The alcohol seemed to be wearing off. Damnit! I should have thrown this at him while he was piss drunk!

"What do you think I wouldn't understand?" I continued. I was starting to sound like a whiny little child and I didn't like it.

His exasperation was building. "Just leave it alone, okay? This has been our arrangement and it will stay our arrangement. You can't just go changing the rules."

"Why not?" I argued. "The rules have changed; our relationship has changed. Everything has to change now. This isn't fair."

"You know what? Don't fucking lecture me on 'fair' right now."

I scoffed, "Says the successful businessman to the red light district stripper."

He jumped to his feet and grabbed his pants. "You know that's not how I see you."

168

"Really?" I replied, faltering to my feet beside him. "How would I know that? I know nothing about you and you know everything about me!" I groped blindly around the floor for my two-piece and pulled my clothes back on in a huff.

"Christ, Navaeh, why are we talking about this right now? Everything was fine..."

"Fine for you, maybe. But you didn't fall in love with some kinky stranger you don't know from Adam!" The words careened out of my mouth with the velocity of a jet liner and the charisma of a three-legged cow. There had been no chance of stopping them, and there was certainly no taking them back now. In a matter of seconds, I had flipped the entire game on-end.

What, in the name of Jenny's sociopathic ex-heroine dealer, was I thinking?

I considered taking the blindfold off right then and there, evening the playing field, but I feared I might lose him forever if I made that mistake. So I waited. And waited. And waited some more. I waited until the sound of those beloved footsteps disappeared into ambiguity behind the lifeless sound of the shutting door.

I removed the blindfold, but the room was still dark, deadened by the piercing axe of loss that had just split my heart in two. Once again, the fog was closing in and heaven was irretrievably out of reach. I didn't want to go anywhere. I didn't want to leave the room. So I didn't. I rested my weary body in a fetal position on the cool floor and waited for the tears I knew had already been spent. My body dry, my brain numb, and my spirit buried beneath a heartless garbage dump, I pretended I could disappear.

Chapter 20

I thought I was done that night he left, I really did. I figured I'd still be curled up on that floor a week later, a starving, and decrepit mess. But the funny thing about struggle – you can only fall so many times before you say, "fuck it" and start trying to remember how to live. The only other alternative is suicide, and that simply wasn't on the menu for me. So I peeled myself up off the ground and opened my eyes for the first time in months: what was I living for?

Turns out, I had a lot of really great things to live for. I had my family, fucked up as they may have been. I had Jenny's scandal, which was pretty high on the list of 'Awesomest Revelations I've Ever Had', securing a spot just above the time I did pot and 'realized' I had exactly ten thousand hairs on my head. I had my job. I had my friends. Most importantly, I had my writing. And no matter in what bullshit ways life tried to drown me, I could always turn it into something useful: a magazine article, a story, a poem. The possibilities were endless. This sparking light bulb made more difference to me than any other psychological or self help concept ever had.

Of course, my problems didn't disappear. I was still beyond terrified that someone might discover my secret. I kept waiting for the phone call from the police explaining that the remains of a human being were found in the trash can behind the club and that I had been connected to them. I kept waiting for Tommy to come to his senses and decide never to talk to me again. More than any of that, though, I was afraid I'd never be able to forget. The memories were still firmly etched into my brain: The smell of burning flesh, the eyes popping unnaturally out of his forehead, the feeling of his breath on me while I stood terrified and powerless against the wall. No inspirational moment could soon wipe that from my mind.

But even though I couldn't let go of everything, I could live. I could work, write, and enjoy the company of my friends. I started to find minutes during the day when my mind was completely clear of my worries and guilt. Minutes of bliss, they were. Minutes that became treasures.

A few weeks later I even chanced a stab at a girls' night. Mia, Candy, Anna, and a few other girls decided to take Friday night off and hit the Strip together. I couldn't remember the last time I'd gone out with friends to just relax and have fun so I enthusiastically agreed to go along. I was so excited that I took a trip into the city to shop for an outfit.

"Can I help you find something?" The lady at the boutique looked me up and down, no doubt taking my mental measurements.

For a moment I regretted my choice of cutoff shorts and a ratty t-shirt, but it was Vegas; who was going to judge me? "I'm going out Friday night – a girls' night. I need something sexy but comfortable."

171

She grinned broadly. "Wonderful! I'm Greta and I've got just the thing. Follow me." She led me to the back of the store to a series of racks sporting all sorts of trendy dresses and skirts.

I started thumbing through them one by one, but quickly became overwhelmed. There were so many. I'd never been much of a shopper and this experience reminded me why: I hated choosing.

Luckily, Greta seemed to live for it. "Let me start you off with a few suggestions based on your body type and complexion."

I heaved a grateful sigh and stood still as she loaded my arms up with dresses.

The next two hours were spent laughing and giggling with Greta as I tried on outfit after outfit, some of which looked utterly ridiculous and others which had considerable potential. About halfway through our giggle sesh, I stood in front of the dressing room mirror, sporting a short strapless black leather dress with chains decorating the bust and a chain belt around the middle.

Greta suppressed a chuckle.

I glared in the mirror, gripping the tail end of the belt and swinging it around in a threatening manner. "You'd better be careful: I'm willing to bet this outfit has a machine gun and handcuffs stuffed in the bra."

We both burst out laughing and I dove into the dressing room to the get the hideous thing off me. Soon Greta was purposely bringing me the most awful outfits she could find and I had a great time practicing my acting skills.

I grimaced as I stared at myself in a short little number feathered in deep green chiffon with an open slash across my middle that exposed my belly button. Lacy green fabric cascaded off the empire waist in random spots creating an almost Mary Magdalene type look.

"I don't think I'll be able to eat any fruit if I wear this one," I giggled.

172

"Um, if that's what Eve wore in the Garden of Eden, I may just become religious again."

I snorted. "We should start a church that requires its members to sport sexy little dresses like this. We'd never have a problem collecting offerings."

At last, as the sun dipped behind the fall clouds, I found the perfect one. It was a deep maroon with spaghetti straps and a flare skirt that reached just a few inches below my little butt. The empire waste had one sexy little bow and the skirt was decorated with tiny beads that hung just off the edge of the seam.

"That one really brings out your eyes," Greta commented.

"I like it a lot. I'll just have to make sure I don't bend over."

"It's Vegas, honey. Unless you're planning to hang a tail of one hundred dollar bills out your ass, I don't think anyone will notice."

I made my purchase along with a pair of adorable satin stilettos in a matching color, and called it a night.

When I got home, I slumped exhausted onto my couch and turned on the TV. It occurred to me that I had just gone three full hours without a single thought of my mysterious stranger. A pang of regret struck my heart as I remembered him walking off after I confessed my love for him. If only I had kept my mouth shut...

I pushed the thoughts from my mind. If I forgot about him for three hours, I could forget for three hours more.

In the midst of my depression I'd gotten a little behind on politics so I settled in with some popcorn and a bottle of wine for an evening of news debates. One of the local channels was holding a discussion regarding Vegas criminal activity and its connection to the economy. I turned up the volume as several political pundits sat at a

173

roundtable discussion with a few of the up-and-coming local candidates. I was immediately transfixed.

Three glasses of wine and two bags of microwave popcorn later, I was yelling at the TV and throwing popcorn every time a Republican candidate's face came on screen. It was genuinely satisfying and I felt as if I were in the midst of them, telling them why they were idiots and where they could shove their social ideals.

I could do a strip tease in the middle of the table, I thought as I took another swig from the wine bottle, *That would shut the fuckers up.*

"We have to remain vigilant in fighting crime, no matter the implications on the economy. We simply can't imagine that immoral behavior can lead to stability. If we start with the base of the problem, the rest will correct itself," explained Jeff Dunn, one of the Republican pundits.

I threw a three pieces of popcorn at the screen. "I'll show you vigilant," I muttered.

Boswell piped in. "I don't think it's that simple. In fact, I don't think it's ever been that simple. We have to keep our eyes on crime – yes, absolutely. But we need to use a strategy that works. When we try to solve a problem by starting from a perspective of fundamental ideals, we lose sight of the end-game we're shooting for. We need an integrated strategy, one that takes a baseline understanding of what these criminals are doing and how they're using the economy and politics to build wealth and work from there. We have to start with intelligence which means authorities and undercover agents on the ground infiltrating these cartels and sects."

"He shoots he scores!" I cried, pumping my fists in the air as I stood. I know – I treat politics like a basketball game. So sue me. "Thank you, Boswell." I clasped my hands in front of me and bowed.

174

The camera moved on to someone else. Boswell returned moments later with another speech so I downed my last glass of wine and swaggered towards the TV (my new TV was huge – as I imagined Boswell was too...). I licked my finger and dipped my ass seductively to the floor, dragging my wet finger across his face on the screen. "You know you like it, baby. You've got all the right stuff."

I turned around and twerked the TV, pulling myself on the couch and humping it like my stripper pole. "Look over here, honey. This is your reward for being awesome." I giggled to myself as I worked through another move in my strip tease.

I stopped short when a question was directed at Smith Anderson – I didn't want my seductive dance to bleed into his low level commentary.

"What's your take on this, Anderson?" she asked.

Anderson looked uncomfortable and shrugged. He seemed out of sorts as if someone had interrupted him at a funeral. "Well...I," he stumbled momentarily, "I take the Republican stance on the issue, as usual."

Everyone, including me, sat stunned. He was blowing off the question?

"And what is that?" the host questioned.

Anderson sighed and ran his hand through his hair. "Look, all I can say is that, though I believe everything must begin with values..." he hesitated. He was clearly walking a fine line. For a moment, it seemed as though he might completely derail his political standing.

I was so confused and it wasn't just the fog in my head from the alcohol.

"You know," he continued, "I'm just going to leave it at that. Everything must begin with values. But there are many ways to define values

175

and many different types of values – take these criminals in the sex trade, for example. They are clearly working from a sense of their own personal definition of morality, which differ from those of most of the general population. I'm not sure we can hope to manipulate their actions without understanding their frame of mind."

The host's face tightened. "Anderson; are you saying you agree with Boswell?"

Anderson shifted in his seat. "It's important for all politicians to be able to work across the aisle, but no, I'm not necessarily agreeing with his approach. I'm just pointing out that this whole issue needs a change of perspective."

Holy fuck. Not only did he successfully evade the question, but he implied (with plausible deniability, of course) that he might have some more liberal viewpoints. I was stunned. The conversation continued, but the host never directed anymore questions to Anderson. It was just as well – Anderson still looked distracted and lost. For a moment in time, I felt bad for him.

"Well, cheers to one politician who might be opening their mind." I raised my glass. "But Mr. Anderson, you're going to have to do a whole hell of a lot more to merit a strip tease from me. For now, you still get popcorn." I flung two more pieces at the screen.

176

Chapter 21

A little dab of lipstick, a spray of my favorite perfume, and a quick shot of tequila. "I'm ready to go."

I took one last glance at my adorable dress in the mirror and decided that it needed a necklace. I pulled open the drawer and retrieved the elegant but indie-style piece Tommy had gotten me so long ago for my eighteenth birthday. It had always been good luck; I wore it for my first kiss, my first sex, and even the first time a boy asked me to go steady. It had charm; a simple multi-layered piece with a few finely crafted wooden beads sparsely scattered across the silver wire and a simple red ruby (that happened to match my dress perfectly) in the center of a daisy at the crest.

A car honked outside.

"Coming!" I called.

I grabbed my red bag – which unfortunately, did NOT match my dress but oh well, Vegas – and my black jacket and keys and ran out to Candy's car. My exit from the house into the cool crisp autumn air merited several whoops from the open windows of the small blue Kia.

"Yowza! Here comes tonight's entertainment, ladies!"

"Somebody wants to get laid!"

"Seeeeeeeeeexy – can I take you home, baby doll?"

I couldn't contain my grin as I slid into the back seat next to Anna. "Why did you ninnies let Mia take shotgun?" I whined.

Mia twisted around to give me an intimidating look. "You feel like fucking with me tonight, Nevaeh? Because trust me, girlfriend, it will *not* be pretty."

Candy pulled out from the curb. "Yeah, Mia just got laid so she's got more smack down than the cartel at a raid."

Mia punched her hard.

"Hey! That's gonna leave a mark!"

"It'll teach you and everybody else a lesson, is what it'll do. Anyone else have somethin' to say?"

The silence was so palpable it echoed.

Mia turned back around. "Okay, pussies, let's go show Vegas what this city is all about!"

The night was incredible. We turned heads everywhere we went – between Mia's hot pink skintight dress, Anna's stilettos with a very visible snake running up the heel, and Candy's head-to-toe body glitter, we were pretty much a free show for anyone who happened to walk by. We laughed raucously, yelled at each other, and messed around with the other crazies along the Strip.

When we'd had enough stranger socialization, we took over a craps table at one of the casinos, drawing a rather animated crowd and a few very excited fellow players. As usual, Mia took center stage, entertaining the crowd with her quick wit and giving everyone at the table a *very* good start when she convinced everyone to bet on

178

a hard twelve and then rolled double six's. We had a pretty good streak going for a while there; our earnings seemed to trend endlessly upward.

Our eager audience included four cute guys playing the table with us. Just when it seemed like we might each be pocketing five hundred bucks from that one game, Mia suddenly announced, "Okay, I'm out!".

We all looked at her, bewildered.

"Are you fucking crazy, Mia, we're on a roll!" Candy cried. Her shyness seemed to be curbed by the pile of chips in her rack.

"Nope. It all goes downhill from here, I promise." She pulled her chips and started for the slot machines.

I chased her down thinking maybe she was upset, but she had a grin on her face. "Mia, come one, what gives?"

"First of all," she said, pulling me in like a confidant, "As soon as six is played after a two, I always quit. Hot Guy #1 just rolled both those numbers so I'm out. Trust me, the game will die. Second of all," she gestured to the four guys at the table, "I want to find out how interested in us those guys are. If they like what they see, they'll walk away from the game and join us over here. If not; we'll find some other hotties to flirt with." Damn, she was good at this game.

"Wait, what about you and Randy?"

"What about me and Randy? He doesn't give a damn who I flirt with, and he certainly doesn't care if I save a few bucks by letting guys buy me drinks."

She continued on to the slot machines and I headed back to the girls, unsure what to think of Mia and her crazy relationship. I motioned to Candy and Anna to come with me and we all joined Mia at a group of machines surrounding an image of a Porsche.

179

"All right, ladies, you're learning from the master," Mia began.

Anna glowered, clearly not convinced that her fun deserved to be quashed.

"Those nice boys over there are headed this way right now. You ladies wanna get laid tonight? We gotta ignore them and stay on the machines until we find out how hard they're willing to work. Trust me – this is how you get the hottest guys in Vegas."

We looked at each other and slow smiles spread across our faces. Considering we spent most of our work hours flirting shamelessly for the attention of far less attractive men, giving these guys the chance to woo us was a temptation far too great to ignore.

We took a seat and, as Mia predicted, they sauntered over with all the confidence of an LA boy band.

"Ladies…" the blonde boy lilted. "Nice game playing over there. Why'd you leave so early? You were like our good luck charm."

Candy batted her eyes and grinned up at him. "Well, how sweet are you?"

Mia shot her an evil look, but Candy was far too busy giving googly eyes to blondie.

"Sam," he introduced, offering his hand to Candy.

"Hannah," Candy announced, offering her dainty hand which Sam took occasion to kiss.

I almost threw up a little bit in my mouth.

"The other guys are Ben, Darryl, and Johnny." The two brunettes and a nice, tall, lanky guy who looked to be some mix of Asian all nodded coolly towards us.

We smiled and waved.

I always had a thing for tall, lanky guys so I gave a little extra eye to Johnny before turning back to my machine. He seemed to appreciate the

180

gesture and I could feel his gaze on me as I seductively pulled the lever on the game.

"So what are your plans tonight, ladies?" Sam asked.

We turned to Mia who just smiled. "We haven't decided yet. We're waiting for a couple of hot guys to come up with something fun."

They all grinned.

"Well, this is Vegas," Darryl said, his interests clearly set on Mia – poor guy. "So whatever we do, it has to start at the most expensive club on the strip."

Mia lowered her head and looked up at him through her lashes, her lips forming a subtle kiss "Now there's a guy who knows how to make a girl swoon. You've got connections?"

"Great ones." He glanced around the room and leaned in with a nod. "You'll have to see it to believe it."

Mia looked him over skeptically before hedging her bets. Her eyes still trained impartially on him, she nodded at us. "You bitches in?"

We giggled and nodded.

It was almost humorous how we each meandered towards our man of interest as if it was some sort of important secret. Johnny put his arm around me right away and led me through the casino and out to the strip.

"Where are we headed?" I asked.

"I have no idea," he laughed. "But Darryl has connections everywhere. He wasn't kidding – he's taking us somewhere good."

I smiled. "Wow, you're lucky to have such a friend."

He looked down at me with sparkling eyes. "Yes, I am lucky."

After shoving through a few crowds and the boys showing off by catcalling a few pimps, we walked into The Venetian.

181

I gave Johnny a playful nudge. "Come on now; anyone can get into The Venetian."

Darryl overheard. "Yeah, but not everyone can get into Tao."

I raised an eyebrow. The guy had confidence. It remained to be seen if he had the contacts to back it up.

We walked up a set of ludicrously ornate stairs and then rounded the corner into a darker hallway. Crowds of people spilled out of the club, waiting for their turn to get past the bouncer. We pushed through, the thumping hip-hop music blasting more and more deliciously as we neared the entrance. Darryl had a conversation with one of the bouncers who pulled out his phone. He talked to someone momentarily, asked Darryl a question, and Darryl responded by raising eight fingers. The bouncer scowled, but waved him through.

I started jumping up and down. "Oh my God! We got in!"

Mia put her hand on my shoulder to temper me. "Honey," she yelled, "this is one of the most exclusive clubs on the strip. If you don't stop bouncing like a schoolgirl, they'll show you the door as quickly as they opened it."

I immediately stood stock still – still anxious, but rerouting my excitement to my fingers which I tapped on my thighs.

"Nervous?" Johnny asked, lacing his fingers with mine.

"I don't get to do things like this every day," I admitted.

He smiled and winked. "Well, get ready. Things are never boring with Darryl."

I almost squealed with delight as we walked in to find a large golden bathtub filled with sparkling water and gorgeous flowers. In its colorful depths, two scantily clad women washed each other seductively.

182

I couldn't help but pull Candy aside. "I think I just found the one job that would be more fun than stripping!"

We both giggled with delight and followed our group through to the bar. Darryl ordered a round of some very fancy looking drink that I can only assume was some kind of high class martini. We stuck it out by the bar at first, unsure if we could handle a crowd that likely had millions of dollars wrapped around just their fingers. After a couple of drinks, Candy and Sam were all over each other already and Anna was not far off so Mia suggested we all hit the dance floor. And, of course, we pretty much always do what Mia says.

Johnny was getting more and more sexy by the drink so I pulled him out to the floor with me. They still didn't know we were strippers so this was our chance to show off some of our best moves – and it appeared we didn't disappoint.

As the night progressed, the high class establishment became more and more like a high school kids' basement party with people knocking each other over and drunken groping like I'd never seen before. Johnny and I had a pretty good grind going but I'd been a little more shy than usual. I could tell it was starting to irritate him because he kept trying to pull me in for a kiss only to land on my cheek. I didn't know what my problem was; I liked him, I just wasn't anxious to jump into heat with a stranger. Well, *another* stranger…

As midnight rolled around, I gave in to his advances and our lips met for the first time. My drunkenness allowed me the creativity of mind to pretend he was my beautiful stranger and before I knew it, we were making out in a dark corner of the club. We certainly weren't the only ones. Even Mia had disappeared to add a little spice to her evening.

Johnny was far more tender and passionate than I expected. His lips caressed mine gently and

183

he worked his fingers under my short skirt slowly and seductively. I unbuttoned his shirt and ran my fingers over his chest, delighting in the bumps of his ribs and the roughness of his chest hair.

As I jumped up and wrapped my legs around him, I couldn't shake the eerie feeling that I was being watched. I glanced around in all directions while Johnny trailed kisses down my neck, but nothing seemed out of place.

Must be the alcohol. It's making me paranoid.

Johnny's tongue slipped beneath my dress and licked my barely-covered nipple, sending a wave of ecstasy through my body that washed away all concerns. I moaned and released my legs, returning them to the floor so I could fiddle with his belt buckle.

He leaned down to my ear. "Shall we take this somewhere more comfortable?"

I smiled and nodded but caught sight of Candy walking into the bathroom. Johnny pushed me up against the wall, his teeth nipping at my neck.

I retaliated gently. "I've got to...I'll be right back..." I was having a hard time thinking straight. "...I need to meet Candy in the bathroom."

He didn't seem to hear me as his hands slipped all the way up the back of my free-flowing dress and he pulled me into a deeper kiss.

"Johnny, wait." I pushed him back again. I didn't want to be a pain in the ass but I needed to get caught up with the girls before I went anywhere. "Johnny, let me go, I have to go talk to Candy."

"I'm not done yet, baby," he breathed into my neck. "God you taste good..."

I started to worry I was going to miss Candy altogether so in a last ditch effort, I pinched his nipple.

184

He cried out and stepped back but didn't let me go. "What the fuck are you doing?" He massaged the spot where I pinched him.

"I just need to go to the bathroom first…" I mumbled.

He backed me up against the wall again. "You can go to the bathroom when I say you can go to the bathroom."

"Johnny…" I started smacking his shoulders with my hands, unsure really how that was going to help the situation, but then he disappeared. Well, it seemed to me that he disappeared.

I heard a scuffle next to me and jerked my head to see a mess of blonde and black hair flying through the darkness. The fuzzy scene was followed by a loud thunk and a shout that sounded like Johnny.

I looked around me to try to understand what I was seeing but everyone else seemed just as shocked as me. I finally caught Mia's eye – she was in Darryl's arms just feet from us and seemed to be motioning to me. I didn't understand what she was doing.

By the time my foggy brain directed me back to Johnny, he was on the ground by himself, clutching his bloody nose and moaning. I fell down beside him to attempt to inspect the damage.

Mia was by my side in an instant. "It was him, Ellie, it was him!"

My eyes lazily made their way to hers. "It's Johnny. I know; it's Johnny. He's hurt."

"No. Focus for a second. The guy that hit Johnny – it was him; it was the guy that keeps buying dances at the club. The guy you're in love with!" Her words didn't register at first and I just stared. "Wake up, for God's sake!" she slapped me across the face, the sting ringing much more painful than I expected. "Go get him; he's probably not too far!"

185

Finally, her words registered. My beautiful stranger had been there. I flew to my feet with no concern for the state of my date and bolted through the crowd. Well, I tried to bolt. I probably meandered and fumbled, maybe even stumbled a little bit. I did eventually make it out of the club and down the stairs to The Venetian. But my stranger was nowhere to be seen. Not that it mattered. The futility of my efforts hit me when I realized I had hardly recognized Mia when she was just feet from me at the club – what were my chances of being able to recognize the ghost of my beautiful stranger?

I slumped defeated on the couch in the entryway, concern for my safety or my potential company completely lost to me. I shut my eyes.

Chapter 22

Two things took me by surprise when I awoke. One: I was in my bed, wearing my pajamas, and didn't have some freak lying next to me. Two: three objects sat on my bedside table, all three of which had never been in my bedroom before. The first was a glass of orange juice, the second was two pain reliever tablets, and the third was an envelope with my name on it. I glanced around nervously as I picked up the white envelope, afraid I was about to open a court summons. What if someone had found out about it and decided to blackmail me? For a moment, I didn't want to know what was inside that envelope, but curiosity got the better of me. I tore off the seal and pulled out a note and ticket of some sort. I spread the note in my lap, took a deep breath, and began to read.

Dear Nevaeh,

I know that's not your real name, Ellie, but I still like it. I'm sorry I ran off on you a few weeks back.

All our weeks of fooling around suddenly became real and I needed some time to think. I meant it when I said I need you – this past three weeks has been torture. I had hoped I could leave all this behind, but then I saw you at Tao last night with that man. I know it's immature, but it become clear to me that you mean more than I had anticipated.

I hope I didn't cause any permanent damage to your friend – no, that's not true. I hope he rots in hell. But either way, I've made some decisions. I want us to have something more and that is something I cannot do under my current circumstances. I've been contemplating leaving it all behind since before I met you. Now I know I want to walk way, but I want you to come with me. I know it's crazy, but crazy is the only thing that has worked for me these past few months.

Enclosed in this envelope is a plane ticket to Iceland. You told me you wanted to go there, remember? We can do this, Ellie; we can start over. I'll explain more on the plane, but, if you meant it when you said you loved me, please meet me at the bench at the far end of the concourse on October third. It only gives you a week, but I sincerely hope to see you there.

– Your Strip Club Fuck

I know what you're thinking: *Um...what? Didn't he run out on you? You know, after you acted like a complete turd and told him you loved him? This is a joke, right bitch?*

No. No, it's not a joke.

The note was real. My beautiful stranger had not forgotten me, quite the opposite, in fact. He wanted me the same way I wanted him. My heart raced as I tried to decide if I was elated or terrified. The funny thing is, this scared me more than the worrisome note I had concocted in my head. Doesn't that seem completely insane? Court, testifying, prison...I'd seen enough crime dramas to know those weren't events to look forward to, but

188

running off to Iceland with a stranger? It was an idea containing no inkling of sanity. And yet, as I sat there pondering the note, turning the plane ticket over and over in my fingers, I knew I couldn't *not* go. I mean, maybe I wouldn't actually get on the plane; maybe, I would go to meet him and then make my decision from there. But either way, I would be at that airport bench, ticket in hand.

It was already late afternoon and I had to get to work so I set the envelope delicately on my bureau and set out to pull myself together for the day. As I jumped in the shower, it occurred to me that my beautiful stranger had been here – in my house! He must have found me on the couch at The Venetian after I passed out and brought me back here. It was relieving to know he had been there in a moment of such inane stupidity; surely I could have fallen victim to a far less ethical character had he not been there.

I stepped out of the tub, dried myself off, and reached for the phone. If he'd brought me home, did Mia, Anna, and Candy know about it? Were they wondering what had happened to me?

Mia picked up on the first ring. "Well, hello honey cakes, how was *your* evening?" she sang.

I groaned. "How am I supposed to know? I just woke up a half hour ago. The only thing I remember before that was passing out on the couch at the casino."

I could almost feel Mia's disappointment through the phone. "Well, that's not very interesting."

"Tell me about it. Mia, please tell me you saw him. Do you know who he is?"

She laughed. "No, but apparently everyone else does."

"What does that mean?"

"How the hell should I know? I followed you out to the casino and saw him lift you from the

189

couch. I figured you were in good hands for the night – no, not just good hands. Ridiculously sexy hands. Seriously, Ellie. Oh. My. God. You are one lucky girl."

"Really? He was that hot?" I couldn't help the squealing timbre to my words. I felt like a schoolgirl again.

"Uh huh. I thought about talking to him but I was afraid I would try to steal him from you."

"You've already seen him before, haven't you? Why are you acting like you don't already know what he looks like?"

She huffed. "Well I only saw him at the club and I couldn't see him very well. I told you he was cute, I just didn't know *how* cute."

I smiled to myself. *And he wants to run off with me.* "So you were saying about everybody knowing him?"

"A lot of people were stopping him to talk. It was kinda funny, actually. He kept trying to help you off the couch, but then someone would approach him and he'd jump backwards like a scared cat. I got to watch a good fifteen minutes of that entertainment before he grew a pair and told everyone to go to hell so he could get you out of there."

"Did you catch a name?"

"Oh come on, Ellie, I was smashed. I almost slept with Darryl, I was so smashed."

Damn. The mystery remained.

"But nothing happened? He didn't stay overnight or anything?"

"No…" I opted not to tell her about the envelope. It would ignite an inquisition of the caliber of Guantanamo Bay and I just wanted to get to work and get the next two days over with so I could go meet this gorgeous man and, hopefully, fuck him into the Icelandic sunset. "I gotta go, Mia. I'm working tonight." I hung up before she could protest.

190

And here I am. Happy now? I told you the whole story, down to the very last detail and despite it all, I'm still sitting here at eight-fifteen in the evening with no handsome billionaire, no plan, and most importantly, no clue if any of this was even real in the first place.

If you haven't learned to hate me by now, I sure as hell hate myself. This phantom plane I was supposed to board with my phantom stranger takes off in five minutes and there's no sign that anyone in this airport is here for the purpose of sweeping me off to Iceland to relax, fuck, and build a new life.

I slump further down on the bench and take one more inventory of the people nearby. Potential candidates for Man of My Dreams: an old man sitting at the bar, sipping a beer and poking fun at the cocktail waitress; the cute bartender who is on his way out – damn, I had hoped he was just playing coy with me – and the old lady I harassed who is getting on her plane. There's a young couple in the gift shop, no doubt buying presents for their adorable kids back home. The way the man is grabbing his girlfriend's ass, I think I can be fairly certain he's in a committed relationship. Over at the nearest gate is a frazzled woman sitting amongst two fighting toddlers. A few seats down is a large man typing vehemently on his laptop, eyes glued to the screen. Can't be my stranger; my stranger was lean. Very lean.

Lean enough to eat...

I think it's high time I start taking mental inventory of all the alcohol I have available for consumption at home. If I'm going to have to deal with the disappointment of going back to work tomorrow instead of having drinks with a gorgeous man at the bar of an ice castle, I'm going to need a lot of ammo. I pick up the paper I've been hauling around and give it a glance in a last ditch effort to curb the pangs of heartbreak threatening to

191

incapacitate me right here and now.

Chapter 23

She's finally picking up the newspaper. It's about fucking time. She's been carrying it around all night! So many times this evening I've thought my goals here were going to be left unattained, but at long last....

I hold my breath. The cinder block keeping me cached from sight has been a lonely companion this evening. I've hated leaving Ellie like this, waiting and wondering. She's been here for two hours now, thinking I would show and continually disappointed.

Of course, all of this could have been avoided if she'd just opened the damn paper.

When I left her that note, I really didn't know if she'd take me up on my offer. All I knew was that I had to get away. And after her admission that she, uh, loved me, I knew there was a teeny tiny chance I might be able to take this little slice of heaven with me. I know, I'm a sappy little twit, booking the trip to the very destination she longed to visit. Sappy...or manipulative. With the kind of jackass I've become over the past few years, it's probably the latter.

But if she's willing to jump off the bridge with me, I'm not going to say no. No, I'd take that fine ass anywhere. My neck twitches as she looks more closely at the paper. Hang in there, buddy, you'll be satisfied soon. I hope. It all depends on....

See, I've been fucked over before. Women usually know who I am right away and the response I get is usually pretty easy to categorize as gold digging. With my current marriage in shambles and the divorce sending piles of paperwork through my already-cramping signature hand, women are popping out of the woodwork.

So I have to know. I have to know if it's about the money for her. She must know I do well – she'd be an idiot not to and I'm quite certain she's not an idiot – but the rest of the package – the fame, the paparazzi, the idolization – none of that is coming with me. Most of the money is staying behind too. And considering how clear she has been about her hatred of politicians...I have to know how much these things matter. The only way to do that is for her to find out on her own when I'm not around to sway her reaction.

And I have to be here to see it.

Will she sport that wicked smile I see so often? Will she be unconcerned? I secretly hope for the second response. I don't know how I will deal with it if she's into possessions and fame. I just can't stomach those things anymore, but...I sort of feel like I need her, in a way. And I can't have her if she needs those things.

Shut up, you piece of shit, or go find yourself a tampon to wipe your tears with.

She's looking at the front page, browsing like it's any other day of the week. I hold my breath as her brow furrows. She pulls the paper closer to her face, the picture I've been waiting for her to

194

analyze ripe and clear in front of her.

She looks confused. She puts the paper down as if deep in thought. Her expression melts into worry. She picks it back up, her eyebrows tethered. My hands are sweating profusely. I run my hand through my hair.

A look of shock palpitates her visage. I can't breathe. I haven't been able to breathe for minutes, it seems. This is the moment of truth.

Her face falls into her hands – I can't see her expression. Is she crying? Laughing? Happy? Tired? When she lifts her head, the scene that unfolds before me freezes me into a state of shock.

*   *   *   *   *

I have never ever, ever been so pissed off. Not once in my entire life. Did you see this coming? Is this the ending you anticipated? Because if so, I'm seriously going to kick your ass.

My head is buried in my arms, partly because I'm trying not to cry and partly because I have this overwhelming feeling that I've been hoodwinked. I keep waiting for a TV host to jump out and say, "You're on Candid Camera! Will you tell us how you feel about this exceptional joke we just played on you?"

That's how this feels: like a fucking joke. It can't possibly be real.

It was all too good to be true. Why hadn't I seen that before? This shit doesn't happen in real life! Of course not, and here's the proof sitting right in front of me: today's newspaper with a picture on the front page of a politician speaking in front of a large and adoring crowd, photographers and supporters everywhere, his right hand raised high in the air as he waves to his fans. And on that right hand is the most chilling sight: half his middle finger is missing.

"I lost it in a steel mill accident," I recall him

195

saying.

A steel mill accident.

A FUCKING STEEL MILL ACCIDENT. ARE YOU KIDDING ME?

I read through the article, perhaps as some kind of masochistic torture tactic, I don't know. It's the same political bullshit he always spews, only now it hurts more deeply. I crumple the newspaper, shove it in the trashcan, and leave the lifeless bench. I need to think.

I storm into the bathroom like a hurricane and pound my fists on the wall. How much time wasted? How much love lost? How much hope flushed down the toilet for this douchebag man – a married man, no less – who pretended to be a good person I thought I could love?

No, I can't blame him. It's my fault. My own fucking fault for being so stupid, like a preteen in pigtails walking around with "Anne of Green Gables" tucked under her arm. Yep. At twenty-four, I'm officially a thirteen-year-old.

Look, it's not like I didn't know that utter and complete failure was a possibility here; I knew my dreams were likely to be shattered, but I didn't expect this. Not for one moment did I anticipate that the beautiful stranger I'd fallen so hard for would turn out to be someone I despise; someone who stands for everything I hate; someone of such decrepit moral character.

I guess that's why he didn't show up, the bastard.

Maybe I should give him a break. He is a politician and politicians get wrapped up in the game just like anyone else. Maybe it's not their fault they're assholes.

I smirk to myself. This is how much I want to love this man. This is how much I want this to be real: I'm willing to stretch far and wide for a justification that makes this right. I'm willing to dive into the depths of my ethical sense of what is

196

right and what is wrong to justify his world for him. In no other circumstances would I ever fall so far.

I splash some cool water from the bathroom sink on my face and glance up in the mirror. It's time to face the music: mistakes like this can't happen anymore. Something has to change. I have to change.

But what do I do now? Do I just hope he never shows up at the club again? Do I hope that he does? I feel torn in a million pieces. On the one hand, I'm pissed off beyond recognition. On the other, I don't want to let go of this man, this wonderful person who has embraced me exactly the way I am. He was willing to leave everything behind for me – presumably. Hell, he took me into his arms, knowing what I've done and knowing that I have more secrets. Worse secrets. He was willing to play his cards, take his chances on me.

I touch the scar on my face. It always feels worse – bigger, bumpier, deeper – when I'm upset. As if it grows in tandem with my despair.

And then it hits me: I was face-to-face with him. I stood right in front of him and I had no idea! My mind races back to that moment in the bar, the bloodied politician at my side nursing his facial wound, and his lame attempt to protect me from my livelihood. Then the confrontation at the amphitheater, the look of shock on his face when he saw me. I had interpreted his surprise to be due to my political leanings, but now I know better. He knew exactly whom he was standing in front of.

I treated him horribly. Yet he still came back…

And despite my anger and frustration, here I am, stroking and acknowledging this part of me that I haven't been able to face in years. I turn my face so I'm staring directly at my right cheek. Tears fall heavy across the faded scar. This is part of me. This is who I am. It's a part of me just like being a

197

stripper is part of me. Just like killing and burning the Pot is now a part of me. Just like...

I peer closer as a sense of recognition fills me. The jagged crevices where the stitches once sat hold memories. They're faded and distant, but still there. They feel so familiar, so close. I can almost feel the pain of the wound as I reach towards the mirror to try to grasp them. My fingers brush the glass as if touching a lost and imprisoned version of myself.

Like lightening, images flash through my mind. Horrific nightmares – me, a young teenage girl, under the control of insidious old men. They hold me down. They force me. They get angry when I resist. Even worse, some of them seem to enjoy my resistance. The faces of several men plague my brain, flashing through like a torturous slideshow, faces I can see clear as day.

"Such soft skin," They purr. "So pretty"...

One in particular keeps reappearing over and over and over. He stands by the door, collecting bills as the others approach me, leering.

Holy fuck. It's him.

My knees buckle and I have to grasp the countertop to keep myself upright. He's in my head, everywhere. Dark and evil flashbacks of him plague me. They've been plaguing me for as long as I can remember, stuffed beneath the veil of survival and ambition. He's the one who started all this, who stole my life at such a young age. I've never made the connection before – I was far too blind, far too lost. His face tortures me as the memories of him handing me off to pedophilic offenders come stumbling back like lost, limping wolves. At eighteen years old, I thought I was free of him. I thought I'd never see him again. I expelled him from my psyche with such force that I didn't even recognize him when we came face to face.

"I think I'd like a special treat tonight, Miss Titty."

198

I watch the pain trickle down my face and away from my soul. It was no coincidence that he left me so incapacitated. It's no surprise that I attacked him so passionately and violently. It was completely sensible that I delighted in watching him melt away into nothingness in such a depraved and worthless manner. His demise was a celebration, a profound ceremony to acknowledge my newfound freedom.

He deserved it. He deserved every fucking moment of it.

I stare for ages. It feels as though I'm watching old Ellie melt away with my tears, and glorying as new, determined, no bullshit Ellie breaks through the grime. I've spent so many years running, so many years hiding from her. I didn't think she was strong enough. But she is. She can face the past. She can move forward.

I lose myself in that dirty mirror for an eternity, watching the real me slowly return to its long-lost place. Passengers come and go. Some of them stare. Some of them ask if I'm okay. All I can do is nod. I hardly know they're there. It's just me right now. Me and my past, standing off in a final battle of wills. I have a lot of work to do; a lot of writing to do; a lot of faces to identify. This is how I move on. This is how I begin to heal.

As the clock strikes ten, I finally pick up my red purse and secure it over my shoulder. It's time to return to my life. It's time to walk forward complete, whole, and unafraid.

I leave the bathroom with only a half-hearted glanced at the bench that carried me through this awful night, the bench that has a piece of me tattooed into its skin. I pause, eyeing it from a distance through my lowered lashes. Can I really walk away so easily? Did I not splay all my hopes and dreams into that one object, that one spot that once held a future in its sadistic hands? I walk slowly back over and run my fingers over the scratchy wood surface, feeling the groves that represent my pain. It's hard to imagine that I haven't somehow left a small part of myself here. As if my spirit will forever wait here in optimistic hope while the rest of me tries to move on and forget. I don't want to be split, two different people hanging onto two different futures. But I can't take this moment in time with me. I can't take any of it with me.

Fine. I shake my head and walk down the stairs towards Passenger Pickup to hail a cab. Ellie is back, but wimpy Ellie who lives in denial, Ellie who hedges her bets on one rotten egg, she can stay on that fucking bench. Maybe she'll never leave. She may rot there until she melts into the hardened surface and becomes a weathered version of anger and heartbreak, but the rest of me? The parts that I care to keep? We are divorced from her, violently ripped apart like an escapee and her tethered arm. Badass Ellie is boarding the ship, prepared to captain the raging seas, any resulting victims to be left behind in decay.

I'm ready. Ready to be who I really am. Ready to chase the past down the dismal hallway of malicious men, armed and predatory. Ready to forget about the person I was when I fell in love with the cheap bullshit politician, Smith Anderson.

Chapter 24

I stare down at the bright white sheet of paper crisp and clear on my desk. My pen is poised, ready to continue the list, but my heart is tight against my chest, a dull ache that radiates through my body.

I take a deep breath and release it slowly as I count. "One, two, three, four, five, six seven, eight…"

Eight men I can remember. Eight of them are etched somewhere in my brain. Eight of them rip my already ragged heart into tiny, jagged shards of glass that tear into my insides like a chainsaw. Maybe I can't do this; maybe I don't have the stamina. I've been here almost the entire night and still I only have two names on the paper.

Dennis Clifton
Alex Pryer

And I'm already out of energy. I have no strength left to continue. I want to give in; my emotions have received enough punishment for one night. I'm so emotionally drained, all I can do is dream about being at the club right now, losing myself in the music, forgetting about the world, the heartbreak, the past…

Tap, tap, tap.

At first I think it's my imagination. I've only slept four hours since returning from the airport; hearing things is certainly not beyond the realm of possibility. But then it comes again.

Tap, tap, tap.

Hours of criminal research have me on edge and I reach for the gun in my purse. If there's anything I'm feeling right now, it's the desire to beat the living hell out of anyone or anything that might even have a passing thought about taking advantage of me.

The morning light creeps over the hills and through my front window as I cautiously approach the door. It's too early for packages, neighborhood children, or visitors. My paranoia is sky high, but I don't care. I'll be paranoid forever if it will protect me from living through that again.

Without a sound, I line my eye up with the peephole.

I recoil. On my porch stands a very scattered, very dejected Smith Anderson. I toss the gun on the side table. What the fuck is he doing here? He was supposed to meet me at the airport not ten hours ago. Did he forget? Is he here to gloat about his cruel joke?

He must be here to explain – hell, he'd better be here to fucking explain. I've died and come back to life over past twenty-four hours and I have nothing left but a teeny tiny morsel of hope that there is a reasonable explanation any of this.

I try to feel angry but my emotions have run dry. All I can feel is…

Relief. Huh. Not what I was expecting. I mean, the relief I feel that there's no attacker on the

202

other side of the door? That makes perfect sense. But I also feel strangely relieved that he is here. My beautiful stranger. For the first time, I can see him.

In a moment of intense impulsiveness, I suddenly don't care who he is.

Emotions are boiling up in me faster than I can control them. The memories of that need, that compulsion to have him next to me holding me, sucking in my bad feelings, his body pressed up against me, is suffocating. I can hardly think straight. After everything I've remembered – the teenage nightmares, the awful, old, ugly, disgusting men, the reality of who the Pot was – I need to be held, kissed, and fucked so badly I can hardly breathe.

Before I can argue, I throw the door open.

He looks at me with pleading in his eyes. "Ellie! Thank God."

He looks beautiful. The morning sun adds a lighter luster to his brown hair, softening his appearance. His green eyes pierce just like they did in my dreams. A light, feathery button-up shirt hangs lazily across his chest over a pair of faded oh-so-sexy jeans.

He's here. At my door. Gazing at me with an expression that cannot come from a person who so cruelly misled me. My skin is alight with goosebumps and adrenaline pumps through my veins as I stare at my long-unseen treasure.

He shuffles awkwardly on the front step, his hands shoved in his pockets, his gaze meeting mine through his sunken brow. "Ellie, I'm so sor–

Before he can finish his apology, I grab a fistful of his shirt and drag him across the threshold. My arms and legs are around him, my mouth suckling his like sweet honey. I don't care what his excuses are right now; I don't care if he's a total and complete ass. I need him like I need blood flowing through my veins.

His arms are grip me just as tightly, his tongue moves with mine, and his hands explore me every which-way as he backs me up and slams me down on the couch. If I had my head about me, I'd regret last night's clothing choice of old, paint-stained sweat pants and a dirty tank top, but all that matters to me right now is the fusion of our bodies; the connection of our souls.

He begins to pull away and leans back on his knees, but I rise with him, meeting his mouth with every inch.

He cups my face in his hands and gently pulls me back. "Ellie, please. I don't want to do this if you're angry with me. Please, let me explain."

I shake my head. "I don't care right now. I want you. I need you so goddamn bad." I choke back tears; this is not the time, nor the place. *Just be here. Just be with him, Ellie.*

I enter his mouth again and my hand reaches down to his crotch. He seems lost in me for a moment and I think we're going to fly to paradise after all, but he pulls away again.

"Ellie, stop. Just…stop for a second," he pants. "We have a lot to talk about. You have to feel I owe you an explanation. It's not like you not to."

I mold my fingers across his mouth and give him a stern look. "You're right. And you will explain. As God is my witness, you will fucking explain. But you have to trust me: right now, this is what I need."

He studies my eyes carefully, still unsure, but his gaze falls to my lips. His eyes morph from concerned to determined and his lips attack mine with even greater fervor. He peels my tank top off and lifts me so I sit on the backrest of the couch. He suckles and nips at my breasts, his hands kneading my back in a sensual massage. I fumble with the buttons of his shirt, hardly able to concentrate under the heat of his presence.

204

"Fuck it," he growls and he rips the rest of his buttons apart like a rabid porn star, bringing a smile to my lips, and hunger to my eyes. He caresses my thighs gently just above the elastic of my sweats as I run my fingers through his hair.

I anchor my hands on the top of the couch and raise my hips up so he can remove my pants. He tosses them mindlessly to the floor. His lips and hands cascade everywhere from my neck to my knees.

He pulls me from the top of the couch. I wrap my legs around him again and he swiftly flips over so I sit on top of him while he leans against the backrest of the couch. For a few minutes, I'm straddled buck naked on top of his half-naked body and he's just enjoying me – touching, tickling, caressing, kissing – exploring every inch, every curve, every crevice. I run my hands through my hair, grip the couch behind him, and bite my lip as I enjoy the sweetness of his skin on mine.

When I can stand it no more, I reach for his belt and pull off his pants, diving for his cock. He groans loudly as I lick, suck, and pull at him like he's my last meal. When I've had my fill, I rise up and straddle him once again. He sits forward on the couch and pulls on a condom. The muscles in his chest flex and constrict with each movement.

My body pressed tightly against his, our eyes are deadlocked, he finally plunges into me. He fills my burning, empty spaces with power and pleasure. I pull his lips against mine and our tongues invade each other again, knotting us together as a single gyrating mound of sensual flesh. I come quickly, paying close attention to his hands stroking my back and his cock pushing all the right buttons as I am filled with much-needed ecstasy. I throw my head back and cry out. He takes the opportunity to trail kisses up and down my neck and across my collarbone. He soon comes

205

too, moaning softly. He thrusts hard, his entire body constricting.

The moment fills us to the brim and the world feels perfect. He feels perfect inside me and I feel perfect wrapped around him. I rest my head on his shoulder and the euphoria begins to taper off, allowing our bodies to relax and our breath to slow. He cups my backside with his hands, rubbing his thumbs on my skin and we share a few soft, appreciative kisses. I don't want to think. I don't want to talk. I don't want to do anything but to sit here in this perfect moment.

"Have you slept?" he whispers.

I shake my head slowly so my lips rub against his.

"Me neither. I've been up all night terrified that this might never happen again." He places his lips by my ear. "You mean the world to me."

His hands gripping my thighs, he pulls me up and carries me upstairs. I'm already asleep before we reach the bed.

*   *   *   *   *

I've never experienced such beautiful, invigorating rest. It was the most amazing, most intoxicating sleep I've ever known in my entire life. My dreams floated by like softly glowing clouds. No images of the Pot tortured me, nor did feelings of guilt and rage. I felt like a puff of sweetly scented smoke, dancing daintily through a world of pain and tragedy, dark shadows and unruly creatures approaching me with venom but falling to the wayside like harmless ladybugs. I was unconcerned, almost unaware of any danger. I only cared for the light. I only wished to huddle close to the soothing slumber that had evaded me most of my life.

I double-check my cell phone to make sure it's on and charged. I pull my short sleeved top

206

squarely over my low rise jeans and apply a final dabble of mascara. A snort echoes from the other room prompting me to peer around the bathroom doorjamb – Smith still lies on my bed, breathing deeply. It occurs to me that I might be back before he knows I'm gone. It would be ideal that way, in fact. The thought encourages me and I slip on my boots and grab my purse before heading quietly down the stairs.

I glance at the clock as I put together a bowl of yogurt with granola. It's already three o'clock; we've slept almost the entire day. It feels so amazing to get such peaceful rest, but I can't help but be reminded that I'm on a schedule. I leave a note on the table for Smith in case he wakes – don't worry, nothing dramatic, just informing him that I'll be back around five so we can talk – and head over to my writing desk by the stairs.

I gaze at the piece of paper with the two names scrawled across the left side. Am I really doing this? Is this completely insane? Maybe. But my brain accepts no other option. It hardly allows me to question, in fact. My past needs to be dealt with. As I fold the piece of paper and place it in my purse, two faces flash through my mind; the same ugly, decrepit, leering faces I always see. It sends a jolt of terror through my body and I have to balance myself on the desk just to stay standing. I take a few deep breaths and wait for the panic to dissipate.

This. This is what must end. With this, I can no longer live. I can handle that it happened; I can handle that it broke me; I can even handle that it's fucked me up beyond recognition. But I cannot live knowing what those faces did to my face. I won't chance giving one of them the opportunity to stare me down and gloat, to enjoy the view of the scarred and broken girl they created – like the Pot did. I will make sure they only see me one way: powerful and in control.

My boots make a satisfying click-clack sound on the hardwood floor as I saunter confidently towards the door. I open it, take a moment to enjoy the soft warmth of the sunshine and the sounds of singing birds getting ready to close out the day, and disappear into the light.

Once again, the body was cold and still. This time the heat of the sun burned into her back, only vaguely deadened by the high walls of the back alley. Her heart didn't fill this time, his energy didn't glow. There was nothing to be gained, nothing to redact from the expiring addiction.

The wire cutters came out, as they always did. She linked her index finger with his, placed a thin slice of wood in her mouth and bit down hard. Her screams shattered the reflective puddles cradled by the dirty asphalt as bone snapped and deep red drops filtered through the low water under her knees. She wrapped the stub of her hand in a tight handkerchief and held her breath, hoping that if she felt all the pain, every nuance, in those few seconds, perhaps the agony would run dry.

It didn't. With gritted teeth, she tucked her alien finger that carried the course but glinting diamond under his stiff hands.

"You were my last," she whispered. "I needed you, just as I needed the others."

She stood and gazed at the passing train that reflected across the narrow opening of the alley, many yards away.

"Sometimes it's worth it. To love and to lose. If not so the weaker portion can disappear, destroyed by self-evolution." She glanced at his hands which cradled the small portion of her withering body. "It is with kindness that I fade."

She backed away, step by step, until she broke into final, faultless, blameless, shattered pieces.

Her finger twitched.

208

I hope you enjoyed every intense second of Stripped: Muddy Heels (Book 1). And don't worry, Book 2 is on the way!

If you liked the book, please leave a review on Amazon!

In the meantime, please visit my website to join my mailing list:
www.writersoftherain.com

You'll get publishing alerts, free stuff, and the chance to participate in the writing of my next novel! Join hundreds of others getting a free sneak peek into my next unpublished project!

Be sure to check out my short story trilogy, now available on Amazon:

Losing You
Keeping You
Saving Me

And don't forget to follow me!

Twitter: @freakinjane
Facebook: www.facebook.com/authorjaynedixon
Instagram: @freakin_jane

About the Author

Jayne Dixon has been a lifelong storywriter, poet, songwriter, and shrewd vixen with several published short stories and poems. In addition to kickboxing, rock climbing, and a *very unexpected* interest in pole dancing, she enjoys spending time with her husband and two children in Denver, CO where everyone laughs at her jokes and, if they don't, there's always a mountain to disappear into. Jayne publishes fictional stories, poetry, and songs on her blog: www.writersoftherain.com